Geoff Tristram has been a professi[...] years, working for a diverse range [...] Embassy World Snooker, the BE[...] Ravensburger Puzzles, Reeves, Wi[...] to name but a few. He has created artwork featuring the likes of Jonathan Ross, Ian Botham, Jeremy Clarkson, Alan Shearer, Ayrton Senna, David Vine, and virtually every snooker player of note. You may even have noticed him on TV during the 2008 World Snooker Championship, interviewing the players as he drew their caricatures!

Geoff has also designed hundreds of book covers, advertisements, packaging items, and several record sleeves for bands such as UB40. In the 1980s he designed postage stamps for Bermuda's Miss World edition, the Charles and Diana Royal Wedding, Lake Placid's Winter Olympics, and Spain's World Cup football. Geoff's 'slightly rude and surreal' cartoon greetings-card range, Norman and Brenda, can be found in all good card shops and a few not-so-good ones as well. More recently, his incredibly detailed 'Cat Conundrum', 'Best of British', and 'What If?' jigsaw designs for Ravensburger Puzzles have thrilled and exasperated thousands of fans worldwide.

As if this was not enough, he has now written 14 books. In 2016, Geoff was asked by Stratford-upon-Avon's Town and District councils to create the town's 400th Anniversary Portrait of William Shakespeare, which made him rightly proud.

Geoff's younger brother, David, was Samuel French's Comedy Playwright of the Year in 2015, and has also branched out into film-making with the hilarious Inspector Drake comedies and more recently, Doreen the Movie.

Their lovely mom, Ruby, is very proud of both of them, as was their beloved dad, Len!

A Remarkable Chain of Events

Geoff Tristram

DRAWING
ROOM

First published in 2016 by The Drawing Room Press.

Printed and bound by CPI Antony Rowe Ltd.

ISBN 978-0-9926208-6-8

Cover illustration by Geoff Tristram.

Shakespeare-mask image courtesy of Stratford-upon-Avon District Council.

Edited and proofread by Laura Tristram.
laura.anne.tristram@gmail.com

Buy books online at www.geofftristram.co.uk or contact the author via gt@geofftristram.co.uk

'All's Well That Ends Well'

William Shakespeare

Chapter 1

The Elephant in the Room

It was not really what I wanted to see, or hear, for that matter, first thing on a Sunday morning. I had crawled downstairs to make a cup of tea, which I'd intended to drink whilst reading the previous day's newspaper in bed, when two of my senses were confronted, or maybe a better word would be *affronted*, by what greeted me in my living room. A chubby, male youth of some 18-or-so summers was sprawled across my new Italian leather settee, fast asleep. I mentioned two of my senses, because not only was he offending my eyes, but also my ears. This oaf, name unknown, was snoring with such ferocity that the less secure sections of my plaster coving were shelling from the walls and crashing into the carpet. I have known quieter road drills. For a moment I feared that my entire house would collapse, just like the walls of Jericho did after being assailed by a brass section of biblical proportions. I had visions of it disappearing in a huge cloud of dust, like a '60s tower block being demolished with a controlled explosion. I stared incredulously at this bloated creature, whose lardy body was shuddering violently with every

1

snort, and then called out loudly, in the general direction of the staircase, for my teenage son, James, to shed some light on the situation. James grunted something or other from his pungent bedroom and emerged a few minutes later looking suitably dishevelled, as befits a typical 18-year-old the morning after he has consumed at least ten pints of lager, several shots of cheap vodka and a rancid kebab.

'Oh, sorry,' he mumbled, head bowed in shame. 'That's Nosher,' he continued, as if that explained everything.

'What is he doing there?' I pointed, and added tersely, 'And please don't say snoring.'

'He like missed his bus back to Dudley and I like said it was okay to crash here, as long as he behaved himself and went early before you like got up.'

'Well, he's *like*, still here, as you can see, and I'm up, so could you kindly arouse him and *like* tell him to piss off, if you wouldn't mind? Meanwhile I'm making myself a pot of tea and going back to bed for, *like*, an hour. I want him gone long before I come downstairs again.'

James promised me that his fat friend would be a mere footnote in history before I re-emerged from my boudoir, and immediately set about poking and prodding the human walrus with gusto. The comatose git seemed impervious to all of this and continued to snore with such intensity that I swear I saw the previous night's empty wine glass travel unaided across my coffee table. I made the tea, sighed one of my trademark world-weary sighs, and traipsed back to my bedroom, leaving James to his odious task. I had not read more than ten words from the front page of the newspaper when James called me.

'He's pissing me off Dad!' he began. 'The bloody bloated bugger won't budge.'

Once I'd praised my son for his effective use of alliteration, and then reprimanded him over his gutter language for the umpteenth time that month, I suggested that he should try hitting this Nosher fellow about the face with a shovel, and if that failed to make an impression, jump up and down on his generously proportioned stomach. James uttered something inaudible and continued trying to waken the Sleeping Beast, as I had decided to christen him, after cleverly fusing the titles of two popular children's stories for comic effect.

I had managed to digest the bottom section of the *Daily Mail*'s page 3, where they usually site their dubious scientific/medical breakthrough item (*Can Over-Ripe Bananas Really Cure Bunions?* Short answer – no!), when James called up to me from the bottom of the stairs again, this time with a heightened sense of urgency noticeable in his voice.

'Dad, can you come here quick? He's not waking up.'

I petulantly threw the newspaper onto the bed, hissed an unprintable swear word, and hurried down the stairs. James was sat in the armchair with a face like thunder. I glanced over at the fat oaf, who was still snoring louder than a

3

jumbo jet (if indeed jumbo jets snore), and it immediately struck me that something had changed. Either that or I had been incredibly unobservant during my previous downstairs visit. Nosher now had the word 'TWAT' emblazoned across his brow in broad, black, felt-tip pen.

'What on earth is THIS?' I growled, pointing at the expletive, shakily written in 76-point Helvetica bold caps.

'He was *really* beginning to bloody annoy me so I wrote on his brow,' explained James, helpfully, if explained is the right word. 'I told him he could like kip here if he absolutely promised to behave and leave early, as I said, 'cause I know you hate when my mates use this place as a doss house. You gave me a right bollocking about it last time and I didn't want another one. He's really, really like, let me down, the shit!'

'In fairness,' I sighed, 'it's not actually his fault if he can't wake up. Is he not responding at all? Jesus Christ, James, he could be seriously ill, you dozy sod.'

I had a go at prodding and poking him. There was no sign whatsoever of him emerging from his slumber. I grabbed his fat cheeks roughly and wobbled them from side to side. Again, nothing, other than the ear-shattering sound of his snoring. I offered a silent and sarcastic 'thank you' to my maker, but in a strange way I meant it – grateful at least that the youth wasn't stone-cold dead.

'This is serious,' I announced gravely, my in-depth medical examination concluded. 'We need to ring for an ambulance right now. This isn't normal.'

'We can't have an ambulance turning up and seeing that on his brow,' said James. 'We need to get it off right away.'

I could feel my blood pressure rising.

'You don't say? Maybe you should have considered that before you wrote swear words all over him. Have you got a rare form of Written Tourette's or something, you bloody idiot? What did you do it with?'

James sheepishly showed me the felt pen he'd used. It was my chunky-tipped indelible one – the one I address my parcels with.

'Oh Jesus Christ!' I sobbed. 'That won't come off. Quick, go up to the shed and look for a bottle of turpentine substitute. It looks like water and it should be on the top shelf by the car cleaning stuff.'

James ran towards the back door.

'Wait! See if you can find another bottle near to it. It's a smaller one with a sort of purplish coloured liquid in it. Methylated spirits it's called. And flipping hurry up. I'll call 999.'

I grabbed the phone and rang the emergency services. A lady answered and began asking irritating questions. I thought at one point that I might have to supply her with my inside-leg measurement. Then she eventually got around to interrogating me about the patient's condition. Was he responding to being poked? Was his breathing regular? Had he taken anything? What colour was he? Were his pupils dilated?

James arrived breathless and panting, with two bottles in his hands. I asked him what Nosher had been taking. James said he'd had a lot to drink, but knew nothing about anything else. I gave him a piercing stare. He assured me that none of his associates dabbled with drugs. I believed him. The lady explained that an ambulance crew would be with me in minutes. I almost asked her if they could go the long way round to give us time to remove the word 'TWAT' from Nosher's brow, but I thought better of it. I thanked her brokenly and replaced the phone. Between us, we manhandled the lad off the settee onto my conservatory floor, into the recovery position, like the lady had suggested, and I applied the thinners liberally with a tissue, doing my best to avoid his eyes. It stank. I rubbed at it with my handkerchief but made minimal progress. Meanwhile, James had emerged from the kitchen with a bowl of hot water and some Fairy Liquid. He tried that instead. It didn't work.

I sent him back for a scrubbing brush, and I exfoliated Nosher's brow until I had to stop for fear of turning him into Yorick. Desperate now, I tried the meths. I soaked some kitchen roll in the stuff and rubbed it into his skin, and at last the pen began to dissolve, albeit slowly. By the time we'd more or less removed the offensive word,

Nosher's brow looked as if he'd been sunbathing in Dubai for fifteen hours straight without sun cream. I'm sure I could see his skull through the thin layer of skin that I *hadn't* rubbed away. And he stank like a Siberian chemical factory. I then searched the lad's pockets for any evidence I could find; an empty pill packet maybe, or a card that an epileptic or diabetic might carry – anything that would help the paramedics to diagnose the problem. There was nothing apart from a folded piece of paper. One side had some random Christian names written in biro, along with the sentence: 'The port is under water. Port intended as a gift for mother.' The other side bore the words 'FRAME GARY FOR THE BANK JOB', as well as, 'HE NEEDS TO KEEP HIS MOUTH SHUT', which worried me no end. I absent-mindedly pocketed it, and it was at this precise juncture that the doorbell rang. I dashed to answer the door, opened it, and there, blocking out my light, were two burly police officers. This was not what I was expecting. One of them eyed me sternly and spoke.

'Excuse me, sir. Are you Adam Eve?'

I answered in the affirmative, my voice tremulous with nerves.

'May we come in, sir? I have a reason to believe that you have stolen two olive trees.'

7

Chapter 2

Free to a Good Home

At the risk of destroying the drama and momentum I was building up, I feel we need to briefly rewind to Saturday, the day before I discovered the oaf on my settee.

I was strolling down Eggington Road, where I live, en route to the Post Office, with the intention of purchasing a copy of the schizophrenic *Daily Mail* (one day they love someone, the next they want them flogged and hanged), when I passed a house that had two plant pots, each playing host to a rather threadbare olive-tree sapling, if that's the correct expression (I am no gardener), and onto each pot was sellotaped a small sign that read 'Free to a Good Home'. I ground to a halt and studied this scenario for a moment, and I mouthed the word 'uncanny', because it bloody well was. An hour earlier, I had decided to do something about my backyard. All my neighbours had patios, but it would have been stretching the truth a little too far to refer to my own miniscule and unloved pile of uneven slabs as a patio. I had been idly leafing through a garden leaflet that had fallen out of the previous day's

Daily Mail, and was admiring a small photograph of a pseudo-Italian courtyard, and, being a glorious, early-spring day, it inspired me to give the rear of my small semi-detached house a facelift. I wanted lots of terracotta pots with exotic foliage bubbling out of them, and two olive trees, like the ones in the photograph, either side of a swishy rattan dining set. You can imagine my surprise, upon eyeing two such trees an hour later, yards down my street, begging for a good home. As is often the case in my life, I felt as if someone, somewhere, was listening to my innermost thoughts and looking after me. How else could I explain the myriad coincidences and strange happenings that had befallen me in my 45 years of existence? I marched up the tarmac, emboldened by this latest happening, grabbed the two pots and headed back to my house to deposit them in my garden, hoping against hope that farther down the street I would find an unloved rattan dining set waiting for me.

As you've probably gathered from the description of my house, I am currently not all that well off. I'm a journalist-cum-writer – in truth, more 'local-free-paper hack' than J.K. Rowling – and work had been patchy. I once had a very nice house, as it happens, but now my wife lives in it, thanks to our divorce, seven years ago. We get on fine nowadays, which is a blessing. I just wish we'd got on as well when we were together. It would have saved me £150,000. Back in those heady days, when I worked for a posh, glossy lifestyle magazine, I'd have thought nothing of popping to the nearest garden centre and paying through the nose for two new trees, but in recent times I tended to look for bargains.

I must admit (and we're back to Sunday morning now, so you don't get confused), the sight of two burly coppers at my front door had made my heart race. I had a real emergency going on in my conservatory, and these two buffoons were quizzing me over two lousy olive trees that I had legally taken possession of. My immediate thought was that it was some nosy, interfering neighbour who had dobbed me in after spotting what he or she erroneously presumed was a precocious smash-and-grab raid.

'Are you okay, sir?' asked the tall, ugly policeman on the left. 'You appear to have drained of colour and your eyes aren't focussed. Are you on some form of medication?'

'Erm, if you don't mind, officers,' I stammered, 'it's not convenient right now. Can you come back later?'

The taller, even uglier policeman on the right spoke.

'I'm afraid that won't be possible, sir. That would allow you time to destroy the evidence, would it not?'

Before I could reply, an ambulance screeched to a halt outside my house and three paramedics – two male, one female – leapt out of it, carrying a stretcher and various medical bags. The policemen seemed rather surprised to see them. The medics strode briskly to my front door, and one of them asked where the patient was. I made my excuses to the police and led the medical trio to Nosher,

10

who was still in the land of nod on my conservatory floor. James was kneeling next to him, spraying the aftershave I'd got him last Christmas into the air above Nosher's head, and wafting it downwards with his other hand.

I gave him one of my looks and subtly gestured for him to leave the scene of the crime, using my eyes and one thumb only, so as not to be too obvious. He retreated to the armchair and sat staring at the wall, his hands clasped tightly together. The paramedics stared at him suspiciously for a brief moment and then set about their business, checking the patient's pulse, shining pen-lights into his eyes, and so on.

Behind us, the two coppers stood silently, having let themselves in without a search warrant. They appeared to be biding their time until they could have their turn. They looked perplexed. I'm sure I would have done too, had I been them.

'Bloody hell!' said one paramedic. 'Has he been drinking meths?'

'I'm getting turps as well,' said the other man, who was obviously a wine connoisseur with a good nose.

'Turps and Aramis mixed, if I'm not mistaken,' added the lady paramedic. 'Jeez! This chap is a serious alcoholic.'

The chap who smelled meths piped up again. 'Oh my God, he's got thick green pus pouring from his ear.'

11

'That's just Fairy Liquid,' explained James, colouring a little.

'Excuse me, Mr Eve,' said the taller policeman, suddenly emerging from his reverie and waving his hand to attract my attention. 'It looks as if this is a bad time, and I know these folks have an emergency to sort out, but I'll be brief and to the point. Are those two olive trees on your patio?'

'They are, and I took them from number 7 who were getting rid of them.'

The female paramedic looked up. '7, Eggington Road, do you mean? Just down the road?'

I nodded.

'That's where I live! Are you the bloke who stole my olive trees?'

'I didn't bloody well steal your olive trees,' I insisted.

'Can we deal with this later, folks?' said a male paramedic. 'This chap is in a coma in case you hadn't noticed.'

'Jesus Christ!' I groaned, head in hands.

'You bloody shit,' snapped the lady paramedic, 'and a neighbour as well, as if to add insult to injury!' she added, as she rummaged noisily in her bag. 'The Neighbourhood Watch lady over the road told the police that she had a good description of the offender and saw which house you'd gone to, but I didn't know it was you!'

'Offender? I'm not an offender, madam. They had a sign on them saying "FREE TO A GOOD HOME". How can that be stealing them, for God's sake?'

The male paramedic injected Nosher with something and stared gravely at his male colleague.

'They *were* free to a good home,' the lady continued. 'That's how *we* got them. I'd just collected them from an old lady in Vicarage Road. Then I took them out of my car and dropped them by the garage doors while I went to get some scissors to remove the "Free to a Good Home" signs and, when I got back, the bloody trees had gone.'

The coppers looked at each other for a few seconds and seemed to physically deflate in front of my eyes. They put their hats back on and made for the front door.

'We'll leave you people to it,' said one of them wearily. 'Sorry to have troubled you.'

Chapter 3

It Lives!

Nosher finally woke up a day and a half later, much to our relief. His parents were beside themselves with worry, as you can imagine, and I kept getting flashbacks and an awful nightmare about waking up on a Sunday morning to find a bloated purple corpse in my conservatory with obscure yellow Post-it notes all over it. I'd like to say he was none the worse for his ordeal, but unfortunately that would be untrue. He had memory loss, a chest infection, he couldn't walk in a straight line to save his life, and one ear was blocked, for some reason. Maybe it was the Fairy Liquid. It turns out that the lad was depressed and had swallowed several of his sister's anti-depressants and washed them down with a few gallons of cheap cider. James did not lie to me. He genuinely had no idea that his friend was depressed or had taken the tablets. He thought the reason Nosher kept crying while they watched the television together in James's bedroom was because he got overly emotional about drama. And animal operations. And the news. And toothpaste adverts. And, come to think of it, the weather forecast. Maybe my son is not cut out for a job in detective work, or counselling.

The next time I saw poor Nosher, I asked him what the piece of paper that I'd found in his pocket was. He didn't have a clue. He couldn't remember putting it there, and the strange wording and names meant nothing to him. As to the note on the other side about the bank job, he just gawped at me like a fish that had been socked on the back of the head without warning with a fisherman's priest. He asked if I was joking, but I assured him I wasn't. I hung on to the slip of paper for when his memory returned, just in case Nosh was a Russian spy – highly unlikely, according to my son, who swears Nosher once asked him if spaghetti was a vegetable. The other possible scenario was that he had just pulled off a massive bank heist before slipping into a coma, and the coded words were a form of treasure map. Even more intriguingly, James assured me that the handwriting was definitely not his friend's. This was nicely written – old fashioned, the way elderly people write, and not in Nosher's trademark illiterate scrawl.

The day after the traumas chez Eve, I duly returned the two olive trees, and I'm pleased to report that, once I'd broken the ice and made the lady smile with a dumb joke I'd recently thought up ('Pizza Express have just introduced their festive Christmas pizza, called "The Wenceslas" – It's deep and crisp and even'), she began to see the funny side of our olive tree misunderstanding, and as a form of olive branch, if you'll forgive the pun, she handed one of the trees back to me and said we could share them, which I thought was lovely of her. Then, blow me down, as I was about to leave with the tree tucked under my arm, she suddenly asked me if I fancied a cup of tea, which I virtually always do.

We sidled indoors, and for a few tense moments I couldn't make up my mind if she fancied me or if a cup of tea was all I was about to get. I suddenly got a bit nervous, and started talking too much. I then noticed a fairly awful seascape oil painting over her fireplace. I should point out at this juncture that, although I can't paint myself, I am quite knowledgeable about art and have a lot of books about it, hence my feeling qualified to criticize her taste in wall decoration.

'Where did you get your picture from?' I asked, by way of keeping the conversation flowing while she disappeared next door to the kitchen to crank up the kettle.

'Oh, it's just something I picked up at a car boot,' she replied.

'I can see that!' I said, instantly biting my lip. She laughed out loud.

'You cheeky sod! Are you always so forthright?' she asked, stung by my insult.

I explained that the filter between my brain and my mouth was missing. I'd tried to blag a disabled badge for it so I could park closer to Waitrose, but the council were having none of it so I told them to shove it, by way of demonstrating my disability. She howled with laughter again, I am pleased to report. The tea arrived and she placed the tray on her small coffee table. I refused an offer of sugar and apologized for my cutting comment, explaining that art was a hobby of mine.

'How's the coma lad doing now?' she asked. 'He was in a fairly bad state when we arrived you know. It could have gone either way.'

I cringed at the thought of what might have happened, and thanked her once more for saving Nosher's life, adding that I didn't know the lad at all, and that he was a friend of my son.

'I knew his face from somewhere,' she said, with a thoughtful look on her pretty face. 'I'm sure I've bumped into him fairly recently but I can't think where.'

We nibbled thoughtful Hobnobs together and a slightly awkward silence fell on the room.

'Have you got a family?' I asked. I couldn't think what else to say.

'One ex-husband, now living in Australia, lord help them, and one daughter, away at uni,' she replied. 'How about you?'

'One ex-wife, living a few miles away, one daughter, Lauren, married, she works for a local auction house, one son, James, who you met.'

17

'Interesting,' she grinned.

I didn't quite know how to take that and it caused me to go ever such a teeny-weeny bit red about the face. She just stared at me with her lovely blue eyes and I was aware of the redness deepening.

'You don't want to associate with me,' I smiled. 'I'm an international olive tree thief.'

'Jug and bowl!' she exclaimed, seemingly apropos of nothing. I asked if this was an order, a euphemism, a cricketing expression or a strange form of swearing, which made her laugh out loud. I like a girl who thinks I'm funny. Most of them only burst out laughing when they see me naked.

'Sorry,' she said, running her fingers through her hair in the most wonderful, sensual way – it's surprising how different she looked from how she'd appeared at our previous encounter. The scraped-back hair, glasses and scrubbed face had been replaced by Scandinavian blonde curls, a touch of make-up, contact lenses, and a previously unseen collection of freckles across her cute nose, and I *love* the odd freckle, me. They were probably always there, but I was too busy worrying about a fat lad in a coma to take them in before. It also didn't help matters when she started ranting at me about nicking her pot plants.

'Sorry!' she repeated. 'I meant he was buying a jug and bowl.'

'Who was?'

'Nocker.'

'You mean Nosher?'

'Yes, him. That's where I remember him from. We were at the same car boot in Stourton, down by the rugby club. I'm sure it was him. I saw this seascape painting that you think is shit – well it *was* only £12 – and he was asking the bloke how much he'd accept for a jug and bowl, which he wanted to get for his mom's birthday. If I remember rightly, he talked him down to £2.85.'

'Bloody hell, I hope Nosher's mother knows what a darling, generous son she has!'

'He found a bit of notepaper in the jug, and the car-booter said, "It's okay mate, I'll include that in the price, being as you're chucking your cash around." It made me laugh.'

'Well I never!' I replied. 'I have that very note in my pocket and the words on it are bizarre. The trouble with me is, if I'm given something like that, I can't rest till I've got to the bottom of it. It's the investigative journalist in me!'

I showed her the note, and like me, she was none the wiser. After careful scrutiny she concluded that the jug and bowl's previous owner was a bank robber who'd been sent a bottle of port that should have been sent to his elderly mother, and he'd hidden it in the bath, under the water. I concurred. Great minds think alike and idiots never differ. I stood up and cleared my throat. It was time I made my way home, before the intense eye contact led to something even more intense. I suddenly realized that I didn't even know her name, so I asked.

'Helen,' she said, offering her dainty, manicured hand for me to shake.

'Adam,' I replied. 'Adam Eve – don't bloody laugh, it's a long story, but basically my mom and dad were crap at naming their kids. I have a brother, Steve, and a sister called Evelyn.'

Helen looked at me as if waiting for a punchline.

'Think about it,' I smiled, and walked towards the front door. She opened it for me and we were met with a block of white sunshine, not bad at all for early March. I strode outside, bravely pecked her cheek and mumbled something about going for a drink one night. To my enormous relief, she said that that would be great. It was then that we noticed that both olive trees had disappeared.

Chapter 4

Happy Birthday, Bill!

I was at a serious loose end when the phone rang. I'd typed up and sent my article for the *Stourbridge Gazette* (subject under discussion: the Ring Road – do you loathe it, detest it, or just dislike it intensely?), and I was still waiting for the editor's go-ahead on my piece for *Staffordshire Life* – entitled 'Is There Any Life In Staffordshire?' Now I was jobless and twiddling my thumbs. Actually, I only ever met one person who twiddled his thumbs and that was my dad, so heaven knows how that particular saying became popular. Perhaps it was a '50s habit that's become extinct, like wearing waistcoats and fob watches and taking rattles to football matches. I glanced down at the local free paper and spotted an article about an old lady who had found out that her husband had been seeing another woman, so she chucked his false teeth in the canal. Truth, as always, is far stranger than fiction.

I had decided to either put the kettle on or else drive to B&Q to buy a pair of olive trees and a padlock and chain, but in the end I chose a third option, which was to re-examine the list of names on Nosher's scrap of paper. The note read, in full:

Side 1.

Joan, Margaret, William, Gilbert, Joan, Anne, Richard and Edmund.

I noticed 'Joan' had been written twice, and 'Edmund' had been circled in green biro, with an arrow pointing to a note that read:

Note to self: The port is under water to keep it safe. Port intended as a gift for Edmund's mother.

Side 2.

Frame Gary for bank job. He needs to keep his mouth shut.

I was seriously toying with the idea of trying to find the car-booter now, just for fun, so I could undertake an utterly pointless Sherlock-Holmes-type investigation into this curious note, and maybe find out whence it originated. Well, I didn't have anything else to do did I?

Then the phone rang, which it does so seldom that I jumped a mile. It was a Miss Melissa Missendon, and try saying that after a bottle of Montepulciano d'Abruzzo and three grappas. This exotic creature was the editor of the glossy lifestyle magazine for the Warwickshire area, entitled *The Cutting Edge*. You know the kind of thing – sophisticated dining ('my partner and I opted for the scallops in a matt emulsion with a chi-chi froth and a pea purée smear-test, and it did not disappoint'), adverts for Swiss watches that cost more than a small bungalow, a property section that includes real castles, and a society page where the photographer has arranged toffs in groups of three and four at some upper-crust function, and snapped hundreds of them for us to look at, when surely the only folks at all interested in doing that are the ones in the pictures. Talk about vanity publishing! Mind you, it's a clever ploy, come to think of it. Photograph half of Warwickshire's upper crust and then they simply *have* to buy the magazine to see themselves in it. Genius!

This was the kind of magazine you see on the corner table in a doctor's waiting room, alongside *Yachting Monthly*, *What Car?*, *Country Life*, and *Golf-Bore World*. It's always made up of fifty pages of advertising and one real article, if you're lucky, plus of course the first page, where the elegant editor writes about what a glamorous week she's had, and what went hilariously wrong at her latest dinner party. Such publications make me want to vomit. Melissa purred something about me writing them an article. I said I'd be delighted to.

She explained that I'd been recommended by a gentleman she knew who edited another magazine that I occasionally contributed to. Apparently, he'd told her that my articles were witty and cleverly written. I couldn't help thinking he'd mixed me up with someone else, but I didn't let on. Melissa asked if I'd heard that, on April 23rd, Stratford-upon-Avon would be commemorating the 400th anniversary of the death of our leading playwright, Alan Ayckbourn. Sorry, that was a joke. I meant, of course, William

Shakespeare, no less. She wanted me to write a fairly lengthy 4-page potted history of the Bard for those who didn't know much about him, beginning with his birth and childhood in Stratford, his family's fortunes and tragedies, the move to London, the plays, the meteoric rise to world renown, and so on, and I was to drop in a few memorable Shakespeare quotations for good measure. The article would finish with a chapter outlining the 400th anniversary festivities, which would hopefully whet the appetites of the good folk of Warwickshire, and encourage them to flood into Stratford on the big weekend and make the party go with a bang. I was to contact a lady at the town council for more information about what they had planned – and by the sound of it, it was an awful lot – and then trawl through Wikipedia to get the rest. I thanked Melissa for the commission, which was required within two weeks, and put the phone down. Whoopee! I was employed again, and not a moment too soon. Living life as a freelancer was getting more precarious with every passing year. It is not pleasant never knowing where the next quid will come from, believe me. You might like the sound of it, especially if you work in an office full of jerks, for a boss who makes Hitler seem reasonable, but trust me, it is often lonely and miserable. You begin talking to yourself, which is a worry, and when the work dries up, it is the best cure for constipation known to man.

I abandoned plans to visit B&Q, made a pot of tea, took a deep breath and decided there was no time like the present. I typed William Shakespeare into Google, opened a Word document, and began. I am ashamed to admit that I knew next to nothing about the great man myself, other than a few of his plays which I'd studied at grammar school years back, and genuinely loved. I had some vague notion that there wasn't an abundance of detail about his life available, and not even a reliable portrait of him, but other than that, I was woefully ignorant. Oh yes, and I also remember that he is thought to have died on the same date as his birthday, April 23rd (although, obviously, years later). Now that is a real bummer, especially if they've organized a surprise party at the community centre and you don't show.

The nice thing about journalism is that it allows us a chance to educate ourselves in all manner of subjects, and we get paid to do so. I might have been an ignoramus, but by the end of the week, I was confident that I would know quite a lot. I began by finding out about his parents, and then researching what they did for a living.

They were called John and Mary, such lovely, honest, straightforward, simple Tudor names. I imagined some scholar researching names some four hundred years from now, when folks named their kids V3, XRocket or Warp. He would probably think the world had gone utterly mad, and long for the good old days when people were called Chardonnay, India, Apple, Taser, Summer, Haribo, or Trojan. Maybe even Mary and John were similarly ridiculed back in the 1500s, but somehow I doubt it. Things moved at a sedentary pace back then, and I, for one, prefer it that way.

John Shakespeare was a Stratford glove-maker, if you didn't know, or even if you did. He was also given the job of Stratford's Official Ale Taster (a post my son might well have applied for had he been born a Tudor, judging by his current Saturday night consumption levels), and Shakespeare Senior even got to be mayor of the town, presumably while suffering from a hell of a hangover, but his gloves business struggled later on and he got himself into debt. Times were hard back then, with the plague wiping out thousands of people. There was a high mortality rate, so parents had large families, knowing that some wouldn't make it. I discovered that William was one of eight. They were listed: Apple, Harper, India... sorry, I jest. It was, in fact, Joan, Margaret, William, Gilbert, Joan again, Anne, Richard, and Edmund.

All of a sudden, the room began to swim. I had the strangest feeling of déjà vu. My life was full of coincidences, but surely this was one of the strangest. The list in Nosher's pocket was of Shakespeare's siblings. It just had to be. What were the odds of that happening? I took the crumpled paper from the pocket of my jeans, now its official residence, and stared at it once more. Edmund was circled with an arrow pointing to the sentence about the port being a gift for his mother. I quickly read up on Edmund and discovered that he was the last child, who was probably spoilt rotten by his parents due to the fact that they had lost so many along the way. The first of the two Joans, born in 1558, had lasted all of 2 months. I recalled the line from the poem 'Winter': *And greasy Joan doth keel the pot.* Amazing how I'd retained so many Shakespeare quotes from my childhood studies. A testament to the power of his writing, of course.

Margaret, born in 1562, died aged two. By now the poor Shakespeares must have been beside themselves with grief and worry about how they would fare with future pregnancies. Then came Guilelmus filius Johannes in 1564, as the Latin entry in the Trinity Church Births and Deaths records referred to him. That's Bill the Quill to you and me. Thankfully, for all of us as well as him, he reached 52 before he keeled over. A lousy age to pop his clogs by today's standards, but after what I'd just read, it suddenly sounded on a par with Methuselah by comparison.

Gilbert (born 1566) reached 46 before he decided to shuffle off his mortal coil (one of his brother's better lines, and there were many), Joan the Second was born in 1569, and managed a highly respectable, not to mention quite remarkable, 77. I bet she was interviewed by the *Stratford Herald* on her 77th birthday and she put her longevity down to abstinence from sex and fags and a glass of what does you good each night before bedtime.

In 1571 Anne was born and died tragically young at seven years old, which to me, seems infinitely worse than little Joan's two months, at least from a parent's point of view. 1574 saw Richard pop out of Mary's battered and bruised old womb, only for him to give up the ghost at thirty-nine. Last but not least came Edmund, who apparently found Stratford too dull for his taste, and joined his brother Will in the Smoke as a bit-part actor, only to meet his maker at the age of twenty-seven. If you ever wondered how Shakespeare became an expert on the human condition, folks, I think there lies your answer. He'd lived it.

I took off my reading glasses and rubbed my tired eyes. I rang Helen (yes, she gave me her number too!) and told her what had just happened. She was as intrigued as I was, as you can imagine. I asked what day the car boot was held and she replied that the next one would be the following Thursday. Lord knows how I would sleep until then. I was about to put the phone down when she added, 'I found the olive trees'.

Apparently, the woman over the road had seen the 'Free to a Good Home' signs on Saturday and helped herself. They'd suddenly appeared either side of the lady's front door, so Helen marched over and repatriated them, this time repositioning them in her rear garden. Hopefully that was the last time they would go walkabout, she said. I wasn't as confident. Then she added as a last-minute P.S., would I like to come around for dinner? Nothing grand – pie and chips, bottle of wine, Tiramisu to finish. I gratefully accepted. I tended to exist on TV dinners from M&S, the two courses for ten quid option. Most of the time I'd be pulling something from the depths of my freezer that had exceeded its 'Sell By' by forty years or more. If I was feeling especially lazy I would just suck them frozen like a savoury Jubbly while I watched the box set of 'Breaking Bad' for the tenth time. I know how to live, me. I closed down my computer and took a hot shower to wake me up. I had a bottle of Shiraz that I could give her so at least I didn't need to pop to the supermarket. If I took the scenic route I could get her some flowers from Wollaston churchyard on the way there.

Chapter 5

The Key to a Good Dinner

I turned up at Helen's house bang on time, a bottle of
cheapish Shiraz in one hand, and a small bunch of flowers
in the other – no, I didn't rob them from a grave; what do
you think I am? They were from the petrol station on the
Ring Road. And I'd thought to remove the 'reduced'
sticker and the price. She opened the door looking radiant,
in a flimsy floral dress. It was so cute and sexy that I felt an
involuntary twitch in my Levi's. I hope she didn't spot it. I
was invited in and, once I'd handed over the wine, I
flopped onto her settee and began idly watching
'University Challenge' as we chatted through the wall.
Helen was in her steamy kitchen, doing cookery-type stuff
and looking flustered. She said she'd be with me in a few
minutes. I glanced out of her back window and spotted two
olive trees on the patio. I smiled. Jeremy Paxman asked the
Cambridge team the following question. (I have been
known to invent scenarios for extra comic effect. I swear,
though, this was verbatim.)

'Name the three platonic solids whose faces are triangular.'

The four team-mates were frantically conferring, as if they actually understood the question. I never heard their eventual answer. I was still in shock from hearing the question. Helen trotted in wearing a pinafore, turned the telly off after checking that I wasn't watching it, and slid a CD into her music centre. It was probably entitled Classical Background Crap for Dinner Parties'. That said, it did give the room a certain classy ambiance that pie and chips and a cheap Shiraz didn't deserve, and after we'd downed a few glasses while waiting for the fodder to materialize, things got rather intimate, and without a word of warning I found myself gently snogging the woman on the settee, which was, I have to report, all very wonderful. In between doing this I told her all about the Shakespeare job, and my research, and she told me about some of the weirder happenings at Russells Hall Hospital where she worked. It's amazing how some people are careless enough to accidentally fall onto the vacuum cleaner and get it stuck on their todger. One chap forgot all about the banana he'd left on the armchair for his lunch, and accidently sat on it, naked (he'd been rather hot, it being a good summer), and somehow it had got wedged up his bottom.

We continued this sordid theme over dinner, laughing until it hurt. We interspersed the anecdotes with a little light kissing and much drinking, until, full to the gunwales with pie and Tiramisu, it came to that awkward time of the evening when I either went home or didn't, if you know what I mean. Thankfully Helen clarified the situation by purring something suggestive about me staying over, a comment that very nearly led to premature ejaculation. The only problem was that I'd left the fire on full back at my house, like an idiot (it was, in my defence, only March and it got chilly at night), so I needed to pop home to turn it off, otherwise it would have been on all night and cost me a small fortune. Ordinarily, I could have rung James and asked him to turn the fire off for me, but he'd gone to stay at Nosher's parents' place for the night in an attempt to cheer the poor bugger up a bit, which made things a tad more complicated. Before he left I suggested that he get himself comatose with alcohol and anti-depressants, lie on their settee and snore like a trooper and see how they liked it. The good news was, I had a night off from parental responsibility and things were looking promising.

I gave Helen a little peck and promised to be back forthwith. I tapped my coat pockets to see which one the house key was in. It wasn't in any of them. This was not great news. It appears that, in my rush to get to her house, I had locked myself out of my own. I explained this to Helen and she suggested I ignore the fire and come to bed, but do you know what? I just couldn't, not even in my state of sexual arousal, which probably speaks volumes about me, and almost certainly uses words and phrases in those volumes such as anal, boring, fuddy-duddy, sensible, and 'needs to get a life', to name but a few. I told her I would nip down the road as far as my next-door neighbours' house and take a detour down their drive, over their small gate and into their back garden. They wouldn't know because they were currently on holiday in Benidorm or some such Spanish shithole. I couldn't gain access to my own drive because I had a carport which was locked, so once I was in the neighbours' garden, I could somehow scale the 6-foot fence that divided our properties, drop over into my own garden and enter the house through the long, thin side window of my conservatory, which was, thankfully, slightly ajar. I would be no more than five minutes, and then the night was ours. I would also use this opportunity to feed my pet, Madame Fifi of Wollaston, International Cat of Mystery, of whom more later.

Helen, a keen adventurer, made even keener by the whole bottle of Shiraz she'd just demolished, said she'd come with me to keep me company, so we vacated her premises armed with her torch. As we tiptoed drunkenly down our street, we linked arms and giggled like silly school kids. Once we'd reached my neighbours' place, I did a lot of theatrical shushing, with my index finger to my lips, and we slipped down the drive and over the gate. It was pitch black, and we were both struggling to place one foot in front of the other. Where were security lights when you needed them? Helen's torch, shining brightly as we left her house, suddenly got a hell of a lot dimmer and had died completely by this point. I made some pointed remark about getting Duracell batteries next time, rather than the Poundshop's own brand. I whispered for her to follow me, as I knew the approximate layout of the garden, and I didn't want her breaking her leg on some protruding rockery. One second later there was an almighty *bladoosh* sound, and what felt like a gallon of freezing water splashed up my legs and back. I had forgotten all about their new fish pond. Helen screamed so loudly that several house lights came on simultaneously. It sounded as if there was a murder being committed. This sudden, unwanted illumination allowed me to see her sat upright in the pond with a slimy strip of pondweed clinging to the side of her face. Her lovely floral dress was now almost transparent, and left absolutely nothing to the imagination. She seemed too pissed to care, though it must have been absolutely freezing. She just laughed and laughed, and I started theatrically shushing again, which made her laugh even more. I helped her out of the pond and helped the carp back in, and then gallantly wrapped her in my coat to prevent her from succumbing to pneumonia. Then, in a scene reminiscent of something from *The Bourne Identity* or maybe *Mission Impossible*, I grabbed the top of the fence and tried to pull myself up it. This always looks so easy in action films, but in real life it's bloody difficult. I swear my body is heavier than it ought to be, or else my arms don't have any muscles in them. Either way, I was getting nowhere fast. Then I felt two hands grab my buttocks and begin the push, which was very sensual I have to say. I pulled again, and aided by the paramedic, who I daresay was used to manhandling dead weights, I finally made the summit. I hauled myself onto the top of the fence and then fell like a sack of potatoes, landing I know not where. Helen asked if I was okay, but I was too winded to even reply. It was pitch black once more, now that the nosy parkers' lights had been turned off, but I knew that I'd landed on a rose bush or similar, because I could feel at least 50 fresh puncture wounds in my stomach and chest area. I would be lucky if my blood supply lasted till I could get to my house, and already I was worrying about having enough plasters to stick on all the holes. I groaned and tried to be manly. At least my partner in crime was qualified to tend to my myriad medical needs, if push came to shove.

I looked up, and I could just about see Helen's head, silhouetted against a watery half-moon, as it popped over the fence. The very next second she had landed in my garden with a triple salchow and toe loop, and earned a perfect score from the imaginary Swedish judges. Actually, I think I'm getting mixed up with ice skating there, but you get the idea. She was athletic, and put me to shame. I rose unsteadily, brushing unwanted foliage from my clothing and removing the rose thorns that were still embedded in my torso. I led her slowly down the path to my excuse for a patio, and across the uneven slabs to my conservatory. The long, thin side window was in fact locked.

'I don't get it. That window is ALWAYS open,' I whined.

Helen, who was shivering violently now, replied somewhat sarcastically, 'I q-q-question y-y-your d-denifision of always.'

'James must have closed it before he went out,' I surmised. 'He's very security conscious for one so young.'

'S-s-so what do we do now? I'm f-f-freezing my tits off here.'

I like to think of myself as a decision maker and a man of action, especially when I'm with a nice young woman that I'm desperate to impress.

'I'll smash the glass and let myself in,' I said.

'W-won't that cost you a f-f-fortune?' asked Helen. 'As in, more money than leaving your fire on all n-n-night?'

It was a good point. The downside was that we'd have to then retrace our steps through the rose bushes, over the fence, circumvent the fish pond – suddenly circa £35 for a small, new double-glazed unit seemed reasonable. I felt my way to the small garden shed, which mercifully wasn't locked, and rummaged around, bashing into bikes, flower pots and lawnmowers until I was a mass of contusions, before locating my hammer. I hobbled out of the shed and over to the conservatory's side window, and, offering a prayer to my maker, swung the hammer in the fashion made popular by the Norse God, Thor, wincing a huge wince as I did so. There was an almighty bang. The hammer bounced off the toughened glass and smacked me squarely in the brow. For a brief moment, the black, lifeless sky was illuminated by a thousand twinkly stars, and I was utterly convinced that I was Napoleon Bonaparte. The moment eventually passed, and once more my shivering companion was helpless with laughter. She assured me that this was her best night out EVER. At least that was something to put in the plus column.

I whacked the glass again, and, like the previous t me, it stood firm. Again, house lights were being turned on all around us and I could hear lots of whispering. I called out, 'It's only me, Adam, I'm locked out and I need to break the glass to let myself in!' Cue, more tittering from my soggy companion.

I hit the pane for a third time, and was finally met with a giant crashing sound, followed by the tinkling of glass on the patio slabs. I gingerly slid my arm into the cavity, acutely aware of adding lacerated arteries to my growing list of injuries. I grabbed hold of the brass latch and twisted it open, followed by the stay at the bottom. It was a tight squeeze, but somehow, after first removing the remaining deadly shards of glass from the frame, I managed to ease my body through the gap, and seconds later, I had opened the back door and let my freezing, inebriated playmate in. She was naturally eager to get home and change into something dry, so she headed for the front door while I threw some cat food into a bowl. As I approached my front door, I grabbed my spare key from under the plant pot in the hallway. It had its very own key ring with 'I love Italy' written on it, that my daughter, Lauren, got me from her school skiing trip years back, instead of something more expensive. I left the house and closed the door behind me, jogged down Eggington Road, and caught up with Helen just as she was walking up her drive towards her own front door. Suddenly, she froze in her tracks and looked back at me with a puzzled face.

'What's up?' I asked.

'You know when we shot out of here half an hour back, to break in to your house? Well, I'll cut to the chase, I was in such a rush, I forgot to take *my* front-door key.'

'So you're locked out?'

'Looks like it.'

'You're not kidding are you? Oh shit!'

'Exactly!'

'Do you want me to bust your window?' I asked. I dare not print her exact reply but the gist is that she politely refused the offer.

'Can I stay at yours, and we can sort this out in the morning?' she asked, all doe-eyed. I felt as if I should cuddle her and say, 'There there, my precious baby. I'll protect you!' Instead, I said that she was welcome, especially as James was away. I tapped my pockets to locate the spare front-door key. She still had my coat on, so I'd slipped it into the back pocket of my Levi's. I could feel the hard contour of the key through the denim, which immediately reassured me, for I had become paranoid, but strangely, I couldn't feel the 'I love Italy' key ring attached to it, so I patted my other back pocket and located the key ring and spare key there, meaning that there were in fact *two* house keys now residing on my person. I weighed the situation and decided it was best to keep this latest revelation to myself.

Chapter 6

The Car Boot

I won't go into detail, so you'll have to get your sexual titivation somewhere else I'm afraid. You-Porn on your P.C. is apparently good for that kind of thing, so I'm told. Suffice it to say that Helen and I had a lovely night after the rather traumatic late-evening stage, and we now appear to be an item, to employ the modern vernacular. I *will* reveal that we both woke up hot and sweaty, but that was because I'd forgotten to turn the fire off, even though this was the catalyst for the disastrous chain of events the night before. She had a spare key at her mom's place (and yes, we Black Country folk say 'mom', like the Americans do, not 'mum'), so I drove her there to pick it up. After that she was required at the hospital, so we agreed to meet up as soon as our busy schedules would allow, possibly the following weekend. As seasoned old hands, we were also a tad nervous about things moving too fast, even though we clearly got on like a house on fire, if you'll excuse the rather unfortunate expression. We were both cautious by nature, and there's nothing wrong with that.

I had made a good start on my Shakespeare piece for the magazine, but all I could think of was visiting the local car boot. I'd got a bee in my bonnet about it and, as is my nature, I'd become obsessed and fixated. When Thursday finally arrived, I was salivating at the prospect, and hoping that the man who sold Nosher the jug and bowl would be there. Helen had described his vehicle – a distinctive lime green, battered old van, and as I pulled in to the car park very early that morning, it was virtually the first thing I saw. I strode purposefully over to it, just as the gentleman was laying out his wares, ready for the punters to arrive.

He was around fifty-five years old with a flat cap and Farmer-Giles-style sideburns. He had a ruddy complexion like a farmer too, and around six or seven bristly hairs sticking out of his bulbous pock-marked red nose, which I became oddly fascinated by.

I said good morning and explained about Nosher's near demise (omitting the TWAT on the brow part) and the jug and bowl note. He remembered the chubby lad and wished him a speedy recovery. I said I'd pass on his good wishes. It turns out that the gentleman did house clearances, and the jug and bowl were from a recent one in a place called Snitterfield, Warwickshire. The old chap who lived in the house was a retired professor and a compulsive hoarder. There had been tons of paperwork, battered old plan chests, moth-eaten paintings, tarnished and dented silverware, drawers stuffed with correspondence, camera equipment, a paint-spattered art studio full of materials, dusty frames and so on, and around fifty million mouldy books about

41

everything from Shakespeare to taxidermy, and all shades in-between. The better items had been sent to the local auction house, and the amateur paintings and the cheaper junk he was going to shift through his car-boot operation. My heart sank at the mention of the auction house, but I asked how much of the other bric-a-brac the car booter still had.

'Most of it, to be honest,' he replied. 'Last week was the first time I sold any of his stuff. The rest is in my lock-up in Worcester, apart from a few odds and ends I brought with me today. From memory, so far I've only got rid of the jug and bowl, three flower pots, a crappy amateur seascape and a Victorian brass kettle covered in dents.'

'Can I have first refusal on the stuff in the lock-up?' I asked.

He eyed me as a mongoose would eye a snake. If these car-boot types sniff money they're like great white sharks that have just detected a minute drop of blood in the ocean. They start circling and then suddenly there's a feeding frenzy. I am very aware that I mixed up a few animal similes there, by the way. I was torn between the two so I gave you both.

'Why is it of interest to you?' the car-boot man asked, once he'd finished eying me like a mongoose or shark.

'Oh, nothing to get excited about,' I lied. 'I'm writing an article for the forthcoming Shakespeare celebrations, and when you said he had books about the Bard, I thought they might help with my research. I don't want to rob you of any expensive antiquarian books either. Any old book would do if it contained the information I need. I must admit, I'm also intrigued by the weird note we found in the jug, if I'm honest.'

'Good luck with that!' laughed the man. 'I found drawers jammed full of his bloody notes and none of 'em make much sense. He was eccentric. Half of them are gobbledegook and the rest are reminders to buy cat food or put his recycling bins out.'

He offered me his nasty business card with apostrophes in all the wrong places and asked me to ring him to arrange a visit.

'Well, if the stuff's of no value, I'll bung you a few quid for your trouble. It'll give me something to plough through at night if there's nothing on TV. You never know, he might have been a prolific bank robber in his spare time.'

'Fair enough!' he smiled. 'And meanwhile, here's something else from the prof's house. He was an amateur artist as well by the looks of it. What about this? Harbour scene with lobster pots, £15!'

I grimaced, produced the cash from my pocket, and relieved him of the awful thing. I had to show willing if I was to gain his trust, but I know for a fact that Helen didn't pay that much for *her* masterpiece.

'Can you wrap it up for me?' I asked.

'Bloody hell mate. Your car's only over there, why do you need it wrapped up?'

'I don't want anyone to see me carrying it!' I answered. 'It's bloody shit!'

He gave me a quizzical, puzzled kind of look, which, if translated into words would have said, 'Why did you buy it then, you dickhead?' and then turned his attention to an old lady who wanted to know if he'd knock 25p off a bundle of wooden knitting needles.

I didn't want to seem too keen, so I didn't ring him till the following day. I still didn't quite understand why I had become so obsessed, to be truthful, but I knew I had to follow it through, even if it was a colossal waste of time. Maybe it was the sheer coincidence of it all that fascinated me. I mean, what are the odds of the note listing the names of Shakespeare's siblings, and me finding it in Nosher's pocket just as I needed to research it? I know it sounds utterly pretentious, but I felt that a higher power was leading me somewhere and I just had to follow.

That afternoon, I decided, being as it was a nice day, to visit Stratford and bask in the atmosphere of the place. I had also arranged to meet a lady from the town hall by the name of Caroline Summers, who was going to tell me all about the itinerary for the celebrations weekend, so that I could include the details in my article.

I have to say that the town was buzzing, the sun was beaming down on me, and all seemed right with the world.

Stratford on a sunny day is one of the best places on earth, and there was a spring in my step as I strode into the Hathaway Tea Rooms in the High Street to partake of a lemon drizzle cake and a pot of tea, as is my habit whenever I'm in a nice town. To add to my general feeling of bonhomie, I now had a lovely new girlfriend. Not only was she easy on the eye, but she was good to have around if I needed putting in the recovery position. She'd demonstrated her expertise in that department several times during the previous night.

Caroline Summers entered the café a few minutes after I had been seated by the friendly New Zealand waitress. I knew she was from there because she pronounced the word 'that' as 'thit'. She seemed genuinely thrilled that I'd not accused her of being Australian, like all the other tourists presumably did. I had visited her beautiful country several years previously – hence my familiarity with the subtle nuances of her accent – to return a rare Maori carving to a museum in Rotorua. Those who have followed my career with interest will know all about that particular adventure, which has now become part of Kiwi folklore, so I'm told.

Caroline was a very pleasant, slightly posh, middle-aged blonde lady wearing designer sunglasses. She carried a small briefcase, from which she produced a sheath of papers that outlined the various activities the town was planning for April. It was impressive stuff. The pavements would be twenty deep with visitors from all corners of the globe, she explained, but the key roads would be roped off to allow a huge procession to travel along them, from a muster point near the River Avon to Holy Trinity Church, where the Bard is buried. There would be representatives from many countries, and each country would have its very own flagpole. The flags were to be unfurled by the representatives on a signal, creating a sudden riot of colour. The procession would comprise organizations, schools, well-known actors, civic dignitaries, and the representatives of the overseas visitors. At the head of this happy band was a local school's head boy carrying a quill pen. Every year, the pen in the hand of the Shakespeare bust at the church was removed and replaced with a new one. Presumably all that playwriting was wearing them out. The people in the procession would carry sprigs of rosemary for remembrance, and lay them on the gravestone. A real New Orleans jazz band was being shipped in to lead them to the church, giving the town a carnival atmosphere, and 20 or more camera crews were arriving from all over the planet to capture it. Delegates from towns that shared the name Stratford had been invited to join the festivities – from Canada, the USA, New Zealand, and Australia. Following the trip to the grave, an intimate sit-down lunch for 700 people was being arranged in a marquee the size of a small city. In short, it was going to be a hell of a party. An eminent artist by the name of David Day, from my home town as it happened, had been commissioned to create an official 400th Anniversary Portrait of the Bard, which would be hung somewhere fitting for the good folk of Stratford to enjoy, and remain there indefinitely once the weekend was over. The council had also arranged for 10,000 Shakespeare face-masks to be manufactured, so they could be handed to visitors as they arrived. When the BBC announcer they had hired as Master of Ceremonies declared that it was exactly 11am, visitors would don their masks, so that everyone in Stratford looked exactly the same. It was not the day to pop an LSD tab, I would have thought. Not that I mixed in those circles.

Caroline and I finished our drizzle cake, swigged our tea, and she stood up ready to leave. She had another meeting to attend with the councillor responsible for statues and public art, she explained. These councillors seem to just have meetings about having more meetings in order to discuss future meetings, and never do any real work. Before you call me a hypocrite, I know what I'd just experienced was a meeting too, but at least it was the only one I'd had for a year and it was in a cake shop. The thought of having meetings day in, day out, appals me, it really does.

Being a gentleman of breeding, I allowed Caroline to pay the bill, being as she unexpectedly offered to. I am a stickler for equality, and besides I only had just enough for the extortionate car park by the river. I know this is neither the time nor the place to revisit an old grievance, but ages ago, when my daughter Lauren was a child, my ex-wife and I had paid for two hours' parking by said river, and been delayed by a noisy toddler who desperately needed feeding. Consequently, we arrived back at the car three and a half minutes late to find the most draconian, sadistic punishment of a huge (and I mean huge) fine attached to our beaten-up old banger. In fact, on reflection, the fine was more than the banger was worth. We should have abandoned it and caught the train home. I swore there and then that I would not return – even though Stratford is a gorgeous place – until some genius from the council, or wherever, devised a form or payment machine that allowed you to pay what you owed at the end of your visit, to save you from dashing to feed a bloody meter half a mile away, when you should have been sat in a park feeding a baby instead. I am pleased to see a few more of these machines nowadays. As to my vow to never visit Stratford again after it stung me, well, time is a great healer, as is Germolene.

I had driven from my native Stourbridge to Stratford, an exceedingly pleasant trip (apart from the M42 and M40 of course) that takes you through the picturesque villages of Wooten Wawen and Henley-in-Arden. It was shortly after this that I spotted a sign saying 'Snitterfield – 1 mile', which was where the nutty professor had lived, so I decided to stop off there after my meeting and do a bit of digging, being as I was in the vicinity anyway.

It was to this end that I pulled off the main road later that afternoon and espied a rustic old bugger sat on a bench watching the world go by. I pulled up alongside him and asked him if he knew of the professor who'd recently died, and if so, where he used to live. The man smiled at me, frowned a bit, smiled again, and with a very slow delivery, told me, 'Ar, I knows who you mean. Professor Ridgley his name was, but you're not really starting from the right place to get to his house.'

48

This took some getting my head around.

'You needed to be at the other end of the village.'

'I see. How do I get to the other end of the village then?'

'It's hard to get there from this end.'

'For you, maybe. I've got a car, you see.'

'You might get a bit lost.'

And so it went on. In the end I wished him a good day and risked it. What was the worst that could happen? It was hardly Borneo.

Five minutes later, with no hassle whatsoever, I was at the other end of the village, parked outside a pair of semi-detached Tudor properties in a pretty country lane One was beautifully kept, freshly painted with abundant flower baskets hanging everywhere. An elderly lady was outside on the small patch of lawn, pouring birdseed onto a feeding table. The other house, in stark contrast, looked rather run down. Paint was flaking off the panels between the oak beams, there were no hanging baskets and the grass was long enough to hide in standing up. A 'FOR SALE sign was planted in the middle of what presumably used to be a lawn, bearing the estate agent's name, Pat Selby & Co. I misread this as I pulled up in the car, as 'Past its Selly by', which amused me no end. It doesn't take much, in fairness. I jumped out of my vehicle and greeted the lady, who smiled back at me. I felt sorry for the old dear, living next door to a run-down joint like that. I always think it's a bit sad when one side of a semi takes a real pride in the house and the other plainly doesn't. It's like trying to polish a dog turd, as a friend of mine who works for a local newspaper would say (I think he read a lot of Oscar Wilde's stuff and it rubbed off on him). Whatever you do, half of your building will always look shit.

'Excuse me!' I said. 'Could you tell me where Professor Ridgley used to live?'

'There!' she replied, pointing to the shithole. 'If you're referring to the one who died recently.'

'Is there another one?' I asked.

'Yes, they were twins, both professors, and both eccentric.'

'Well I never!' I replied. 'How did you tell them apart?'

'Oh, that was easy,' she smiled. 'One of them was dead. Besides, they weren't identical, so that helped as well.'

I was beginning to realize that everyone in Snitterfield was barking mad.

'So this dead one, from next door. What was he like?'

She put her birdseed down on the manicured lawn and strolled over to join me at the roadside.

'Well, the expression "nutty professor" springs to mind,' she began. 'Unworldly, and a jack of all trades, master of none, if you know what I mean, apart from history of course, which was what he was a professor of. Used to teach at Oxford like his brother still does until he retired early due to ill health, and then he bought this place, thus ensuring that I'd never be able to sell mine. You're not looking to buy it are you?'

'No, sorry. I presume you mean because of the state of his house?'

'Yes. I know it sounds callous, but in a horrible way I'm pleased he's finally passed away so that hopefully someone with DIY skills will move in and make it look as nice as mine does. Shame he shuffled off before he fulfilled his big ambition though.'

'Which was?'

'Well, I never knew whether he was really on to something or whether he'd just gone a bit doolally. He used to ramble on over the garden gate, a bit like Polonius from *Hamlet*, about how he'd made this incredible discovery. Something that would make him world-famous.'

'Really? Wow! That's interesting. Did he tell you what it was all about?'

'No. It was all very hush hush, he said, and he couldn't divulge it to anyone, not even me, in case I blabbed it out at the Post Office or whatever. As I say, it was probably the ramblings of a madman. The last time I spoke to him, he was waiting for a taxi out the front here. I asked if he was going anywhere nice, and he said he was going to see a chap called Day, but he couldn't tell me about what. I'm sure he said David Day. I remember because it was alliterative. Dennis Day maybe. Something along those lines. The taxi arrived and he jumped in. They drove off so I carried on gardening. Then the taxi pulled up outside again five minutes later, and the taxi driver looked as white as a sheet, which was unusual because he was Indian. Well, they all are nowadays aren't they?'

I was sensing a touch of inner turmoil at this point, as the name she just mentioned was familiar to me, and I didn't think I could take yet another coincidence. I asked why the taxi had returned. The lady suddenly looked a little upset, as if she was struggling to continue without shedding a tear.

'He, erm, he, the taxi man I mean, asked me to help him, so I ran over to the car. Professor Ridgley was slumped over in the back seat, and he was grey. He'd died of a massive heart attack seconds after leaving here. The taxi driver had looked through his rear-view mirror to ask if he wanted to go the pretty way via Henley-in-Arden or straight to the M40, and it was then that he spotted that the professor had keeled over. They were going to Stourbridge, he said, but the poor man was dead before he even left Snitterfield.'

At this point I felt the need to clutch the picket fence, as my knees were buckling.

'And you feel this meeting was what he'd been getting excited about?' I asked.

'That's what it sounded like to me, yes. Now, no one will ever know what he was planning I suppose, unless he confided in this Dennis Day chap.'

'The reason I came today,' I explained, 'is that a chap I know bought a jug and bowl from the professor's house clearance and it had a strange cryptic note inside it. I wonder if you can throw any light on it for me.'

'I'll try,' she said, frowning.

'Well, maybe our nutty professor was planning to retire to the Costa del Sol a rich man,' I continued. 'The note said something about *framing Gary for the bank job*. It also mentioned he needed to *keep his mouth shut*.'

The lady doubled up with laughter at this. Not a reaction I was expecting, if I'm truthful. She took a hanky from her trousers, removed her specs and dabbed her eyes.

'You're not a policeman, come to investigate that are you?' she asked, still giggling. I assured her that I wasn't.

'Gary is our neighbour over the road, just there. The big detached place, and he's a big detached bloke that lives in it, and all. He's the manager of the bank I use in Stratford. Professor Ridgley was a jack of all trades, as I say. He thought he was a bit of an artist but his oil paintings were dreadful. I wouldn't pay a tenner for one.'

I bit my lip.

'He also dabbled in photography, and in fairness, his photos weren't that bad – better than his blasted paintings anyway! He took a picture of Gary at his photography class. They both went to the art and photography classes once a week at Snitterfield Village Hall just down the road, you see. Gary was quite pleased with the result, unlike when the professor had a go at painting him, and made him look cross-eyed and mentally negligent. Professor Ridgley was thrilled that Gary seemed to like it so he made him a frame for it – he dabbled in that as well – and gave it to him as a present to hang in his office at the bank. Talk about a misunderstanding! Sorry the truth is a bit more prosaic!'

I felt myself blushing with shame. 'But what about the bit that said he needed to keep his mouth shut?' I asked.

'Oh, that wouldn't be anything sinister,' she smiled. 'Gary's always had awful teeth, you see!'

Chapter 7

The Hypnopotamus

I had just returned from a rather fruitless and frustrating visit to the car-boot man's lock-up when the phone rang. It was Helen, asking me if I fancied a Saturday night out with a difference. Her friends at the hospital had been to see a comedy hypnotist act in Worcester a few weeks previously, and had been giggling about it ever since. Helen had spotted in the *Stourbridge News* that the same man was now performing at the Town Hall, and she was keen to see what all the fuss was about. She, like me, was deeply sceptical about hypnotism, and suspected that audience members went along with the joke and pretended to be under the influence, rather than spoil the show. You could argue that this in itself was a form of subtle hypnotism, I suppose, in that the performer was banking on them conforming to basic human nature (the lemming syndrome) and endeavouring to fit in. For some reason I was reminded of women faking orgasms, so as not to upset their lovers. We vowed that, if we *did* go to the show, we would both refuse to go down that lemming route. If we were, heaven forbid, called up on stage, we promised not to play along by pretending to be clucking chickens or whatever, just to give the bloke an easy ride. We would be Hypnotism Anarchists.

Some of Helen's friends had themselves been selected as guinea pigs at the Worcester show, and she swore that her boss, a woman who was not prone to making a fool of herself (someone who tended to call a spade a spade, if not a shovel), had delighted her staff by skidding around the stage yelling 'EXTERMINATE!' because she genuinely believed she was a Dalek. Once she was restored to her human persona via a theatrical click of the fingers, she appeared to have had no memory of this whatsoever. I suggested that someone at work should click their fingers one day as they stood near the boss, just to see if it was possible to turn her into a Dalek again.

I assured Helen that a trip to the Town Hall with her would make a pleasant change from sucking a frozen TV dinner while watching 'Breaking Bad' for the umpteenth time, so she scurried off to arrange tickets, popcorn, and so forth. Meanwhile, I looked up David Day's phone number on the Internet. This was a man I was desperate to meet.

Earlier I intimated that my trip to the car-boot man's place had been a waste of time, and so it was, on the whole. I had parted with a few quid to buy the reference books on Shakespeare, and a few other odds and ends, but I couldn't find anything of *real* interest, and by that I mean something that promised hidden codes or hinted at what the professor thought was about to make him rich and famous. Just tons of bric-a-brac and junk really. The nicest and most interesting item, for me at any rate, was a black box file filled with old letters, which I paid the dealer twenty quid for. They looked to be old indentures (not old dentures, thankfully), house deeds, promises to pay back loans and so on, all composed in the flouncy handwriting style of the time, meaning that they were, to the 21st-century eye, utterly unreadable, give or take the odd word. There were letters on paper and legal documents on parchment, with dates ranging from the early 1600s to the mid-1700s, mostly finished with a red wax seal, and either a signature or else a scribble, under which someone had written 'His Mark' or 'Her Mark'. There was also an invoice from an antique shop in Henley-in-Arden for two small paintings 'in poor condition', hence the £150 total – one being an oil painting, probably Victorian it said, of Shakespeare's birthplace in Henley Street. It didn't even mention what the other one was, but described it as, and I quote, 'filthy with tears'. That was tears as in rips, not as in tearful, I presumed. I looked around the lock-up to see if I could find these pictures but with no luck. Maybe the auction house had collared those, but by the sound of them, the council tip seemed a better bet.

I rang David Day's number and waited for what seemed like five minutes, but was probably only four, until someone picked up. I had done my research on this fellow, thanks to a couple of people I know who professed to know him well, and what I heard had made me both excited and trepidatious. The consensus was that he was a thoroughly decent, educated man of some sixty summers who lived in a large barn conversion out near the village of Kinver, a few miles from me. He had, they told me, carved out an international reputation over some forty years of hard graft, as a top fine artist and restorer. My friends also informed me that he was something of a comedian and a scatterbrain and, like myself, an accident-prone chaos magnet, but unlike me, supremely gifted and grittily determined too. Some of his escapades had passed down into local folklore, they concurred, with a series of real-life, rip-roaring adventures that would rival anything written by Sir Arthur Conan Doyle, Agatha Christie, or P.G. Wodehouse. I heard tales of bent international art dealers thwarted and handed to the cops on a plate, impossibly convoluted stories about how David had forged Monets and Botticellis to entrap the villainous Lord Hickman, a local upper-crust ne'er-do-well, and a frankly incredible saga of how David had discovered hidden messages in Michelangelo's Sistine Chapel frescoes, which sent shockwaves through the snooty art world. If only a small part of all this were true, the man was surely a cross between Miss Marple, Stan Laurel, and Leonardo da Vinci, and therefore someone I just had to meet. My friends assured me that we would get on famously, as we seemed more like brothers than some brothers they could name, even though we had never crossed paths before. I just hoped that when he finally answered the phone he wouldn't tell me to piss off.

Just as I had resigned myself to hanging up, he answered breathlessly, as if he'd run half a mile to get to the phone.

In fact, it was at least another minute before I could get any sense out of him.

'Excuse me answering the phone like some kind of heavy-breathing telephone sex pervert,' he eventually gasped. 'I was in the shower when the phone rang and I couldn't find my dressing gown anywhere, so I've had to dash downstairs and answer the thing with nothing on.'

'You're *still* talking like a telephone sex pervert,' I informed him, grinning at my little witticism, 'and I now have an image in my head that I never wanted but don't seem to be able to erase. Anyway, my name is Adam Eve (don't ask, it's a long story), I'm a local journalist and writer, and I have a very interesting story to tell you, if you have ten minutes this week.'

I could tell that this had intrigued him. He confessed that life had, by his standards at least, been a bit dull of late, and he needed a bit of excitement. We agreed to meet the following day at 10am at his house, and he promised to be wearing something, though he couldn't promise that it wouldn't be a basque and fishnets, it being a Sunday. I thanked him profusely and said goodbye. So far, so good. He was approachable and funny. Things were moving along nicely, even though I still didn't have a clue where they were moving along to, or why.

*

I called for Helen and we drove the short distance to the Town Hall and parked the car in Lower High Street. We walked into the shopping precinct that led to the Town Hall's front entrance, and were greeted with garish posters that advertised the evening's entertainment. The Hypnopotamus was well named. If the poster photograph was accurate, he appeared to be around 17 stone with immaculate Day-Glo teeth that looked a size too big for his mouth. This vision of loveliness was enhanced by a purple dinner suit and lavender shirt combination of the type made infamous by Bernard Manning, the brash northern comedian. Either this was meant to be ironic or the man was in a '70s time warp.

We shuffled past the kiosk, showed our tickets and headed for the bar, with its swirling red, blue and violet carpet, or maybe that word should be 'violent'. I wasn't drinking because I had to drive, but already I felt giddy and seasick. I generously purchased a glass of Chardonnay for Helen, while I made do with a rather spartan-looking sparkling water, and we quickly grabbed a free mahogany-topped pub table before the majority of the filthy, unwashed public arrived. Helen had gone down with a bit of a cold, she informed me. By way of proving this to me, she blew her nose and it sounded exactly like that noise the Tardis makes when it's about to set off. Once I'd stopped laughing at her, we began to chat about how we'd got into our respective careers. She said she'd taken the Sciences, Psychology, Sociology, and some other 'Ologies' at school, and always fancied being a paramedic because she could drive around in an ambulance at speed with a siren blaring, and dash from job to job like a superhero, saving lives.

I bet she was one of those kids who asked her mother to make her a red cape, so she could run down the road and watch it billowing out behind her. I told her I'd taken Tautology, Tautology and Tautology at school, but she didn't get the joke, which is a shame, because I made that up myself and I'm rather proud of it. Then the bell sounded, and a voice on the tannoy system told us that it was five minutes until the start of the show. We wolfed down our drinks (which caused me to burp violently for the next hour) and headed for our seats.

Once we were all seated, the lights dimmed and the velvet curtain opened jerkily, to reveal the Hypnopotamus himself, sweating like Tommy Cooper and grinning at us with his outsized teeth. He asked for a volunteer from the audience, and a silly girl in a micro-skirt put her hand up. She was dragged onto the stage and made to sit on one of a row of chairs. So far, so predictable. Helen squeezed my hand, sneezed all over the disgruntled old lady in front of her, and settled back to enjoy the show. Five minutes later, the girl was doing the Sand Dance around the chairs because she thought she'd regressed to Ancient Egypt. It was like Wilson, Keppel and Betty, but without Wilson and Keppel.

Then the Hypnopotamus asked for more volunteers, and instinctively we both shrank by about a foot into our plush red seats. A middle-aged couple trotted up the steps and within minutes they were both acting stupid, one barking like a dog and the other pretending to be a Hollywood actress receiving her Oscar. Helen and I looked at each other and whisperingly concurred there was no way on God's earth that a few suggestive comments from the hypnotist accompanied by a gold watch swinging on a chain could ever render us incapable of rational thought.

'I'm not buying this,' she hissed in my ear, spraying me with mucus from an impromptu cough as she did so. 'It's a put-up job, they're part of his act, surely. I'm not stupid. Do I look like I've got the word TWAT written on my brow?'

'No,' I whispered, 'but I know a place where you could get that done, not far from you!'

She began to laugh, rather too loudly. This brought us to the attention of the Hypnopotamus.

'Ah,' he said. 'I see we have two people in here tonight who are not convinced. Would you pair care to join us on stage?'

'No, you're okay,' I replied, colouring a little.

The irritating folks around us began to prod us and insisted we did. It all got deeply embarrassing, and eventually, due to peer pressure, we shuffled past the people in our row and reluctantly took part. I was made to sit down next to Helen and the big fellow started talking mumbo jumbo at us. I'm not sure if it was because I was mortified by the experience or because I'd caught Helen's cold, but suddenly the house lights felt a little hot and I was clutching at my collar, as if I was about to faint. Then he asked me how I was feeling and

I rallied a little. The audience, I suddenly noticed, were howling with laughter, and I hadn't even done anything yet. Helen too was rolling about on her chair with her hand over her mouth in an attempt to hide her stupid grin. The Hypnopotamus then, rather unexpectedly, allowed us to return to our seats. All around us people were patting me on the back and giggling. I have to say I didn't like it much.

'I told you I couldn't be hypnotized, didn't I?' I whispered to Helen, who was still snorting with suppressed mirth.

'Yes, you did,' she replied, 'and apart from the bit where you declared your undying love for Eric, the penguin cuddly toy, just there on the table, you didn't seem affected in any way.'

I gave her one of my penetrating stares.

'Are you kidding me?'

''Fraid not, buster.'

'And what became of you, prithee?' I hissed, shaken by this latest revelation.

'Nothing,' she said, with a slightly superior, mocking tone. 'I just pretended to go under the ether, and I sat there in silent hysterics watching you act like a complete dickhead in front of all these people.'

At this juncture, her giggling fit became so overwhelming that it was deemed best that we repaired to the bar to purchase a few stiff ones, even if it meant coming back for the car the following day. We stayed there drinking wine and nibbling popcorn until the show ended and most of the audience had long gone home. After that public humiliation, I needed an anaesthetic.

'If ever you invite me to another hypnotism show,' I warned her as I rose unsteadily from my chair, 'I'll be washing my hair that night.'

Helen tried to get up and nearly knocked the table and all our glasses over in the process.

'And if y'ask me,' she slurred, 'I'll be washing your hair as well, so there.'

We zigzagged our way arm in arm back through the precinct past the betting shop, which was still open and full of punters, a sight that never fills me with joy. Then I saw a familiar figure leaving the shop with a scowl on his face. He barged past me, discarding his betting slip as he did so, and vanished into the night. I picked it up and studied it. I don't claim to be an expert, as I've honestly never set foot in a gambling emporium, but to my untrained eye it appeared that our Hypnopotamus friend had just lost around £500, which was probably the exact same amount that he'd worked hard to earn, an hour before.

Chapter 8

When Adam met David

It was probably not the best way to introduce myself, rapping on the window like that. All I could see in the studio was a huge canvas on an easel, so I didn't think the artist was in residence (probably taking time off to brew a cup of tea or whatever), so I knocked on the window to check, and was greeted by a rather miffed looking chap who informed me that he'd just jumped a mile and skidded a loaded paintbrush across Shakespeare's nice white collar. I apologized profusely and meekly entered the room.

'No harm done,' said David in a distracted way, wiping his brush on what looked very much like an old pair of Calvin Klein underpants, and emerging from behind the canvas – like a slightly bewildered mole – to shake hands. 'It's Shakespeare's fault. He's huge and he's blocking out my light. I get the same with the milkman. He taps the window to see if I'm in and I'm usually holding my breath and painting the back legs on a butterfly with a 'triple 0' sable brush. I have to concentrate so much; even the door opening can put me off my stroke completely. It's like open-heart surgery but without the blood!'

I apologized once more, introduced myself, and asked if I could take a sneaky peek at the official 400th Anniversary Portrait. I stood there mesmerized for five minutes. It was breathtakingly good. I told David so and he thanked me.

'I spend days and weeks here in front of pictures, until I can no longer tell if they're any good. You go quietly insane doing this, and this particular one is worse than the others because of who it's of. There's a lot riding on it, as you can imagine. I paint the face on Monday and think it's spot on. I get back in here Tuesday and I think it's crap, so I wipe it off and start again. Come Wednesday, I'm happy with it, but by Wednesday teatime I hate it and it's all wrong so off it comes again, and by Thursday it looks just like it did on Monday, which was perfectly okay in the first place.'

'Bloody hell!'

'Welcome to my world!' laughed David, scratching his nose and leaving a gash of purple paint there. 'Cup of tea?'

I nodded. 'As long as you can spare the time.'

He told me he needed a few minutes away from it. We crunched across the gravel to his house, which was beautiful and had many paintings hanging on the walls, as one would expect. He put the kettle on and we chatted while it boiled.

'So you like it then?' he asked. 'No one apart from you and the milkman has seen it yet.'

'He looks a bit dashing doesn't he?' I asked. 'A bit like Robin Hood or some such ancient folk hero.'

David frowned. 'Yes he does, and I'm a bit concerned about that if I'm truthful. The council are very proud of Shakespeare, as you can imagine, but I think they wanted him romanticized a little. Nobody really knows what he looked like as there isn't a properly accredited portrait of him as such, so we all create our own interpretations – a bit like Jesus in many ways. I'd have preferred him to look a bit more… well, like a normal, everyday chap you might see in the pub or whatever. More believable and approachable, sort of thing.'

The conversation moved on as we sipped our tea, and I told David about my Shakespeare article, and the incredible coincidences that had occurred. I could tell that he was very excited about the car-boot find, and all the Shakespeare links. It was all very spooky indeed. I asked him about Professor Ridgley and why he was coming to see David.

'Ah, that was all very sad,' he said, as his recently dunked chocolate-chip cookie collapsed into his tea. He fished out a huge spoonful of sludge and dropped it into his saucer with a pained look, before continuing.

'He rang me about wanting to see me as soon as possible. He sounded very insistent and promised me something of game-changing importance, which was all very exciting, but he said he couldn't divulge anything on the phone because people could be listening. He sounded a bit eccentric – typical boffin-professor type – and it was fifty-fifty as to whether he really did have something special to show me or if he was just a fruitcake. You have to risk it though don't you? Just in case. Then he doesn't show up, so I'm miffed. I ring him to give him a bollocking for wasting my time and the ambulance people answer the phone and tell me he's died in the taxi. Now I'll never know what it was all about, which is driving me mad.'

I admitted that I didn't have a clue either, but I showed David the cryptic note I found in Nosher's pocket, and told him that the prof's next-door neighbour had also been made aware of some earth-shattering, highly secret discovery. I explained that the name David Day would have meant nothing to me had I not been told of the 400th Anniversary Portrait, by Caroline Summers, the councillor lady that I'd met in the Stratford tea room.

It seemed obvious to both of us, though, that this big secret had to be in some way art-based, otherwise the professor would not be trying to fix a meeting with David. Now, unless I managed to find and decipher more clues from the car-boot stash, it looked as if the prof's great revelation would die with him, a scenario that was exercising both David and myself equally.

We could have talked all day, but David was desperate to finish his portrait in time for the celebrations in April, so we shook hands again, and I promised to ring him if I discovered anything worth passing on. He reckoned that he probably had two days left on the picture, after which it would be touch-dry in a few days. Then he could apply a preliminary retouching varnish and fix it into the rather magnificent Elizabethan-style frame he had had made at great expense. Interestingly, he added that an oil painting was not *truly* dry for at least six months to a year, and only after that could it be varnished properly. You live and learn! Now, if that topic ever arises in the pub, I can wax lyrical as if I have always known about varnishing oil paintings, and pour scorn on those who are ignorant of such things.

We promised to catch up soon, regardless of whether I had anything to report, as we had spent most of our time laughing, and were both agreed that we seemed to have a lot in common, like we'd known each other all of our lives. 'You're like the brother I never wanted!' was David's take on it. We even had cats that could have been siblings, both with the same markings, and both keen mouse-catchers with silly names. His was christened Stevens. It was only when I was halfway home in the car that I got the joke and laughed out loud. Now I was more determined than ever to crack this mystery, and to this end I drove straight home to forensically scrutinize the evidence one more time.

I won't say I'd got a bee in my bonnet about it. Far from it. It was more like an apiary in a hat factory.

*

Helen was away on a course, and James had accepted a kind invitation from his mate Tom's parents to join them for a free week's holiday in Tenerife, so I had no distractions – other than Madame Fifi, my own stupidly named cat bringing me yet another still-alive rodent as a present – and I was determined to make the most of it (the free time I meant, not the mouse). Just in case you were wondering, as I mentioned earlier that my cat, Madame Fifi, is also referred to as the 'International Cat of Mystery', this is because you can search the house from top to bottom, including every tiny nook and cranny, and not find her. Then, just as you think she's lost or has been run over, she appears at the top of the staircase looking nonchalant and devil-may-care-ish, a bit like the Scarlet Pimpernel but with fur. Apologies, I digress; so anyway, I tidied up my Shakespeare article and sent it to Melissa at *The Cutting Edge Magazine*, and then for the rest of Monday I read and reread the bits and pieces I'd purchased from the car-boot man, all to no avail. I was still no wiser about the port being 'under water' and 'intended as a gift for mother', and the old documents didn't look promising. They were what they were. Indentures, IOUs, and the like. Nothing personal or encrypted. The only slightly intriguing note I found read: 'Remember to pop over the road to Gary's house for relaxation session, 4.30pm appointment', which created graphic images in my mind that made me quite queasy. That said, we are all consenting adults with different tastes, and whatever this relaxation session entailed, well, it was none of my business.

On a whim, I decided to ring the professor's twin brother to offer my condolences. Maybe he was even a party to the secret. It didn't seem a hopeful line of enquiry, I admit, because if it *was* a shared secret, he was hardly likely to confide in me, a complete stranger, was he? Regardless of that, I still felt that ringing him would be the decent thing to do, so I contacted his university and asked if he could call me back at his convenience. Surprisingly, he did just that, an hour later.

I introduced myself, expressed my sympathies, for which he thanked me, and I then explained that I'd found the strange notes in a jug and bowl. He was intrigued. I also mentioned that his brother was en route to meet a well-known artist and restorer when he died. Professor 2, as we will now call him for the sake of clarity, was every bit as scatterbrained and eccentric-sounding as I'd imagine his late brother was, but I did get the impression that he didn't have a clue about any imminent revelation, or the trip to see David. He did, however, forewarn me that his brother tended to dramatize situations, and in the past he had claimed to have discovered where King Arthur was buried, the whereabouts of the Holy Grail, and a missing da Vinci painting of great importance (aren't they all?) hidden in a loft in Slough. Sadly, none of these findings had materialized, although the now-deceased professor did once find a Victorian coin while out with his metal detector. I felt my heart sink at hearing this, but I ploughed on regardless.

'Do you know what "The port is under water" or "Port intended as a gift for mother" means?' I asked, fully expecting to hit a brick wall.

71

There was a deafening silence, followed by another one.

'I'm afraid I don't,' he admitted. 'Look, it's nice of you to ring me, Aaron—'

'Adam.'

'Adam, but I really must get back to my next class. Oh, hang on. Did you say port?'

'Yes. As in the drink. Or the harbour of course.'

'My brother often used to write port as shorthand for portrait, when he was dropping me a quick line or an email. As in, "just finished a port of man in our village. V. good likeness", etcetera, etcetera. Could that be it, maybe?' (I noticed Professor 2 pronounced it *et-cay-tera*, the posh, proper Latin way.) I thanked him for his time and promised to get back to him if I discovered anything interesting. Suddenly I had another avenue of enquiry to investigate.

Chapter 9

Eureka!

I sat staring at the wall, deep in thought. The interesting, new avenue of enquiry was looking more and more like an uninteresting cul-de-sac. Okay, so it wasn't a bottle of port for mother. It was a portrait for her. So what? 'The port is under water' didn't refer to some ancient port that slid into the sea like Heracleion, some 1,500 years ago, then. Instead, it was a portrait lost underwater. I was still no wiser. In fact, if anything I was considerably dumber. I continued to stare at my wall. A mouse scurried by. Oh joy! Another one that Madame Fifi had brought in to play with and then forgotten about. I would have to set up the humane mousetrap once more, primed with irresistible parmesan cheese. I watched it dart behind the picture frame that was awaiting disposal via either the charity shop, if they'd accept it, or else the council tip, if they wouldn't. The professor should have stuck to prophesying, or whatever it is that professors do. He was a lousy artist. His harbour looked as if it were constructed of Lego (an insult to Lego which I retract immediately), and his lobster pots appeared to have been drawn by a chimpanzee (an insult to chimpanzees, likewise). And as to the way he painted water...

I stared at the picture for another minute, as the three brightly coloured plastic cogs that make up my brain chugged around in my head. I knelt down beside the picture and flipped it over to reveal the back. Unusually, it was sealed with a sheet of old plywood, which covered the canvas stretcher. This was odd, because if an artist notices that his canvas has become saggy, he can rectify this by tapping the stretcher pegs with a panel-pin hammer to tighten them up again. Even I know that. So why would you nail a sheet of plywood over those? Admittedly, they gather dust, but I couldn't, somehow, see the mad professor being overly house-proud. I trotted into the kitchen and grabbed a screwdriver from the drawer where I keep all the useful gizmos, spare fuses, and the odd woodlouse corpse. I lay the painting face down and began to gently prise the backing sheet off. I felt a little like Howard Carter peering into Tutankhamun's tomb; it was that exciting! Inside, there was an ancient-looking letter, similar to the ones I had purchased from the car-boot man. I opened it, breathing heavily with the suspense of it all. It was obviously something from the 1600s, and had the usual red wax seal. Other than that, all I could see was the canvas back. Then it hit me like a five-ton truck. The majority of the canvas was far, far too ancient to be playing host to the professor's ghastly harbour scene, and didn't match the newer part tacked to the stretchers around the perimeter. With trembling hands, I carefully removed the wooden frame and slipped the canvas out. Using my screwdriver, I eased the staples out of the stretcher and eventually the cheap, new canvas fell off, revealing a filthy, torn canvas beneath. The picture was so black, the man's face was barely visible beneath the grime of ages, and none of his clothing could be seen, save for maybe a hint of a button or two.

It took me several minutes to regain my composure. This could possibly have been one of the two smallish oil paintings that the professor bought from the Henley gallery for £150. But if it was, where was the other one?

I remembered that Helen had also purchased a seascape, and suddenly, it was imperative that I examined it. She was away in London playing at being Florence Nightingale, and I was far too eager playing at being Hercule Poirot to be hanging around till she returned. Luckily, I had trusted her enough to hand her a spare key for my place, and she had reciprocated. I dashed down the street to where I'd stolen her olive trees and she'd stolen my heart (I could easily have another career writing greetings-card verse), and in the blink of an eye I was inside and heading for the chimney breast, like a cat burglar. I lifted her picture off the wall, which I have to say was doing her house a favour, and proceeded to take off the plywood backing sheet with indecent haste. Eureka! I was met by the exact same scenario, except that this time there was no old letter. I removed the frame and then the seascape, but this time I found myself ogling a grubby canvas depicting a typical Tudor or Elizabethan village scene. Despite the place having changed so much nowadays, I still instantly recognized it as Henley Street, Stratford-upon-Avon, birthplace of the Bard. I cleaned up the mess I'd made on Helen's carpet with her Donald Duck design dustpan and brush – funny how insignificant details stick in the mind – and restored the crappy seascape, minus its hidden artwork, before hanging it back on Helen's wall. Then I legged it back to my place with the picture. I breathlessly opened the old letter from my own picture and tried to read it, but the illegible Elizabethan twiddles were beyond my ken. It was like trying to read German. Besides, I knew a man who could read that letter standing on his head. I rang Professor 2 again.

Frustratingly, he'd just that very second begun a two-hour lecture (and they say these university lecturers only work an hour per day), but the secretary, sensing that the call was urgent by my tone (I said 'please' eight times in two sentences), promised me the professor would ring back as soon as possible.

I was far too impatient to sit there waiting, so I used the dead time to drop by David Day's place and hand over the paintings for his expert opinion. It is fair to say that I did not expect what greeted me when I arrived. He answered the front door looking whiter than Banquo's ghost. When I asked what the matter was, he needed to use the nearby wall as support before he could manage to get a sentence out, and for a minute I thought he'd just slither lifelessly down it and collapse in an untidy heap on the floor tiles.

'I've been burgled,' he croaked.

'Jesus Christ!' I groaned. 'What did they take?'

'Only my fucking Shakespeare painting, that's all!'

'What, literally *only* your Shakespeare painting?' I asked, rather tactlessly it has to be said. Surprisingly, he said yes.

'When did this happen?'

'Just half an hour ago. I'd just popped to the Post Office, Suzanne's away visiting her elderly mom and dad, and when I got back it was gone.'

'Did you not lock the door?' I asked.

He gave me a haunted look that penetrated my soul.

'No.'

'Whyever not? You had a painting that was probably worth fifteen grand in there.'

'And the bloody rest. I was only popping out for five minutes, and we never have burglaries or any crime around here.'

'You just did.'

David didn't reply. He just looked distracted and stared into space. I gently prised a paintbrush from his clenched fist in case he was thinking of self-harming with it. I decided that it wasn't the right time to show him the two filthy paintings I had under my arm, so I placed them on his desk and told him I'd explain later. I resumed my enquiries vis-à-vis the break-in.

'Have you phoned the police?'

'Not yet, it's only just happened.'

'Has the burglar left any clues – footprints, fingerprints, whatever?'

'I don't bloody well know do I? I can't remember offhand where I left my Sherlock Holmes Fingerprinting Kit – the one I had for Christmas. There might be footprints in the sand over there I suppose.'

I looked towards the area where the workmen – who had been laying a new block-paved drive – had left a thin layer of sharp sand. Any intruder would probably have entered the premises that way so it was worth a punt. We strode over to take a look, but the sand had multiple footprints, including David's cat's, so it offered little for us to go on, other than a couple of huge ones that looked as if they were owned by a yeti. They must have been at least size fifteens. We arrived at the pavement, and a card and a scrap of paper in the gutter caught my eye. I bent down to pick them up. The paper was an old betting slip. I studied the writing on the card and it caused my head to swim. One more incredible coincidence, and I risked keeling over from a coronary.

The card read:

The Hypnopotamus
A.k.a. Gary Chambers
13 Arden Road
Snitterfield

'Oh, my prophetic soul!' I gasped. 'The smiling, damned villain.'

'Your line?' asked David, dully.

'No, it's from *Hamlet* actually. I think our thief has accidentally left us his calling card,' I announced grandly, 'and I mean literally. He must have pulled his car keys out of his pocket and pulled the card and the slip out with them. What a bloody dickhead! You're not going to believe this, David, but this chap is an entertainer, and my new girlfriend Helen and I went to see him at the Town Hall just this Saturday. What he was doing here is another matter. Who knows about this Shakespeare painting?'

David replied that it was all pretty secretive, as far as he knew. The Stratford councillors knew, obviously, as they'd sanctioned it. I knew of course, but I'd not mentioned it to anyone, not even Helen.

And then there was the address, Arden Road, Snitterfield. That was a coincidence too far, even for me. Professor Ridgley came from Arden Road in Snitterfield, but he had no idea about David's portrait. David had definitely not mentioned it to him, so the professor couldn't have blabbed about it to anyone back in Snitterfield.

'I really need to call the police right away,' groaned David, 'but then it'll probably make the news, and the big, secret Shakespeare portrait won't be a secret any more. I really don't want any publicity about this project until it's launched at the end of April. This is an absolute bloody disaster. Stratford Council will go mad if they find out.'

I stroked my chin, deep in thought. I have never been sure why people stroke their chins to stimulate the brain, but it seemed to work. There are more things in heaven and earth, Horatio, than are dreamt of in your philosophy, I always say.

'Look,' I said. 'I know this Hypnopotamus bloke, I've seen his act, and blow me down if he doesn't live close to the dead professor who was just about to visit you. Something VERY spooky is going on here, and if you let Plod loose on it, it will almost certainly get messy. You said you were bored and your life lacked excitement. What say you stall the phone call to the cops for two hours and drive over to Snitterfield with me, right now, and we'll find this chap. Strike while the iron is hot. He'll still have your painting, so between us we can overpower the bastard and retrieve it. THEN you can call in the police if you want to. The priority is to get that picture back in time for the big celebrations, and between us, we can do it.'

I swear I saw a light come on in David's eyes at this point. He grabbed his coat and a cricket bat, and joined me in my car.

Chapter 10

A Plot is Hatched!

An hour later, we were in Snitterfield, sat in the car outside the late professor's tatty old house, trying to look innocuous. The next-door neighbour popped out briefly to top up her bird table but didn't recognize me, and soon scurried back inside.

Number 13, Arden Road, was immediately opposite the old lady's house, which meant that Mr Gary Chambers, a.k.a. The Hypnopotamus, was also a.k.a. Gary Chambers, bank manager, unless of course two big, fat men both named Gary shared the house, which was unlikely. All of a sudden, things were falling into place. I was wasted as a journalist. I should have been Philip Marlowe. Gary Chambers went to night-school classes with Professor Ridgley and they knew each other quite well. Indeed, the prof. had taken Chambers' picture and framed it for him to hang in his office at the bank. At first the comment about the awful teeth had thrown me. Then it dawned on me that Gary the Entertainer must have treated himself to some serious dental work in the interim, presumably because no one likes a hypnotist with manky choppers. I remembered

Professor Ridgley's cryptic Post-it note about going over to Chambers' place for relaxation therapy. Might this just have been some form of hypnotherapy – the type where you reveal all sorts of things without even knowing you've done so? The only flaw with my otherwise brilliant deduction was that the professor didn't know anything about the council-commissioned Shakespeare portrait that David was just completing in Stourbridge, so how did Chambers find out about it? Not from the professor, that was evident. I was still missing a vital piece of the jigsaw.

Just at that moment, we were interrupted by the arrival of an old, battered Range Rover, which swept onto the gravel drive of number 13. A huge individual got out of the driving seat and headed towards the hatchback, which he opened. David and I suddenly pretended to be reading newspapers, just like all the best private eyes do, peering just over the top of them to see what was going on. It was about as inconspicuous as a tarantula crawling over the Battenberg cake while you are enjoying afternoon tea with the vicar.

Chambers lifted out a large rectangular item that had been covered with a tartan blanket. I saw David's face explode with fury.

'That's my bloody painting,' he hissed, reaching for his cricket bat. I knew instinctively that he wasn't planning to use it for its intended purpose, so I told him to calm down and breathe. There were more ways – I told him, if you will excuse the rather nasty expression – to skin a cat.

Gary Chambers then carried the picture into his house and closed the door.

'We need to get inside there and steal that picture back,' said David, stating the obvious. 'The bloody paint's barely dry. He could ruin it if he doesn't handle it properly. I say we go in right now and beat the shit out of him.'

'And what if he's far stronger than us pair of weeds, or what if he has a gun, or a knife, or a cutting tongue, even? No, the best way is to break in when he's at work, presuming of course that there isn't a Mrs Chambers in there wielding a rolling pin.'

'Agreed,' said David, 'but what if we're seen breaking in to the house and it's us that get arrested? That could get messy, and I bet this little village is swarming with do-gooder neighbourhood-watch busybodies. What we really need is to be invited in legitimately, so we don't have to smash windows.'

'Windows aren't always that easy to break as well,' I added cryptically. 'What about, say, a pair of gas-meter readers?'

'Too dodgy. He may have only just had the meter read, so he'll know we're impostors. Besides, they have proper I.D.'

He fell silent for a few moments, deep in thought. My mates who knew him reckoned this was when he got seriously dangerous.

'I've got it,' he said, a smirk spreading across his face. 'Pest-control officers. I've got a pet printer who'll do us some business cards super quick. If I ring him right away, he can have 'em ready by tonight.'

I gave David one of my looks. 'Are you sure you've thought this through?' I asked, frowning. 'Don't think I'm a spoilsport, trashing your latest brainwave, but what if he doesn't have any pests?'

'Oh, don't worry,' grinned David. 'He will have.'

Chapter 11

Pest Controllers

'Where on earth are we going to get a load of field mice from?' I asked. 'The ones in pet shops are white and domesticated, so they wouldn't look authentic.'

'Do you remember us talking about our cats collecting them?' asked David.

'Yes,' I replied, 'but Madame Fifi might bring two in a week if you're lucky, or unlucky, depending on your point of view, and one of those might well have its head missing. Let's say we average one live one each per week, tops, which means that, combining our cats' efforts, it would take a month to rustle up a minor infestation, you stupid sod! I thought this was urgent.'

'It is *most* urgent,' David assured me, as he fixed me with his mesmerizing stare. 'But I already have a large collection of mice at my disposal.'

I looked at him the way I look at Jehovah's Witnesses when they try to explain the Kingdom of Heaven to me on my doorstep.

'You see,' he continued, undaunted by my assortment of cynical facial expressions, 'recently my oldest friend Laz next door, who also has a cat, bet me fifty quid that his cat, Catty Kirby, Kirby for short, could catch more mice than Stevens could, so every time we had a live one, we rescued it with the trusty, humane mouse-catcher, and put it in this great, big plastic storage thing he's got up the top of his garden. We didn't want to be cruel, because I'm quite fond of mice as it happens, so we agreed that the bet would only last three or four weeks. He made it nice and cosy for them, and put holes in the top so they could breathe, and lots of straw and food and water and stuff – a right little home from home it was, and it's now time to declare that Laz won, the bastard, and for us to liberate them.'

'Hence your pest-controller brainwave?'

'Exactly!'

He showed me the business card he'd had done. I laughed out loud. It read:

Hamelyn & Piper Limited
Pest Control Operatives
Unit 1
Henley Lane Trading Estate
Stratford

'I wrote a few alternative punny names down, such as *End of the Rodent!*, *Good Rodence!*, *Pesterminate!*, *The Verminator!*, and so on, but I thought this one sounded classier. The address is fictitious of course.'

'You are barking mad, David.'

'Possibly. We have a total of 27 field mice. Their habitat was getting far too crowded, thanks to several of them being heavily pregnant when they arrived. We didn't see that coming, I must admit. Now we have a purpose for the little buggers.'

'And what, precisely, do we do next?' I wanted to know.

'Simple, my dear Watson. First, we drop a few cards through letter boxes in Arden Road. Make it look like a proper business, just in case Chambers happens to ask if neighbours had one. Can't be too careful, and besides, the minimum order was for fifty so we might as well use them up. Then, while Chambers is at the bank, no doubt hypnotizing and robbing his customers, we shovel the little critters through his letter box. Leave it a day to see what happens, and my bet is that he'll see the cards, think to himself, *that's opportune, as I have seen a lot of little blighters scurrying about willy-nilly*, and then he'll ring us.'

'And have you thought about *these* scenarios?' I asked. 'A. He never notices the bloody mice. B. He phones another pest-control firm that he's used before, instead of us. C. He disposes of the painting in the interim, or moves it from his house to a secret lock-up.'

David's face appeared to cloud over. 'All fair points,' he conceded. 'Okay, we try it, just for the craic, being as I need some adventure to invigorate my dull life, but we adopt Plan B and call the feds if it doesn't work immediately. As Jeeves used to say to Bertie Wooster, it's all about studying the psychology of the individual, and I'm betting that it'll work, and fast.'

'And if, and that's a big if, he actually rings us, and we turn up in our high-vis jackets - I can't believe you went out and bought two of those by the way - how can I knock on this bloke's front door when he's seen me on stage at Stourbridge? Excuse the joke, but he might smell a rat.'

David gave this some serious thought. 'I have the perfect solution, Watson old fellow. You can borrow something from my beard and moustache collection.'

'You have a beard and moustache collection?'

'Of course. High quality, realistic ones. I use them for reference material. If I need to paint a man with a beard, for example, I put one on my figure model. A made-up one never looks quite right, I think.'

For the umpteenth time that week, I gave him one of my looks. This man was mad, bad, and dangerous to know. A bit like that Lord Byron chap.

We agreed to nip over to Snitterfield that evening under the cover of darkness and hand out the business cards. Meanwhile, I took the opportunity to show David the two old paintings, and he said that he had a bit of a lull before his next project so he would set about cleaning and repairing them right away. I arranged to call for him at 7pm and left him to it. Next I emailed Professor 2 in Oxford and attached a photograph of the letter I had discovered in the back of the painting, in the hope that he could provide a translation. My covering note explained that the paintings and the letter had been owned by his brother and had found their way into a car-boot sale after the house clearance. I added that he was also welcome to test the two oil paintings at a later stage, once they had been restored and the letter had hopefully been authenticated. I reminded him that absolute secrecy was paramount at this stage, due to the enormity of what we had discovered.

It dawned on me as I sent the email that life can be very poignant and sad sometimes. We collect our treasures throughout over many, many years, and then, in old age, we have to decide what is done with them. Those of us who are blessed (and I use the term loosely) with children elect to leave various items to them, but we must remember that they don't always have an affinity with the things you hold dear. Your collection was your passion and not theirs, unless you are extremely lucky. They may wish to hold on to a trinket or two in remembrance of a father or mother, but the rest has no real significance, so of course, they sell it all. How tragic is that? They then set about creating their own collections, only to be disappointed when their own children show no interest. And so life grinds on. It does, on cold and dark winter days, make you ask the question, what's the bloody point?

I daresay that Professor 2 cherry-picked a few personal mementos from his deceased brother's stuff and pocketed the cash from the sale of the other items. It remained to be seen if he'd disposed of and kept the right things.

I don't know how long I sat at the computer in a reverie, pondering the meaning, if any, of life, but I was brought back into the real world by the ping-pong noise that announced the arrival of a new email. It was from Professor 2, and what it said made each individual hair on my neck stand to attention, like quills upon the fretful porpentine (Shakespeare's line, not mine, and he couldn't spell either).

He had read the words on the attached letter immediately, as he had some free time before his next lecture. To say he seemed excited was an understatement, but he had to temper this enthusiasm with the knowledge that letters could be, and were often, faked for monetary gain. He would need to avail himself of the facilities at his disposal in Oxford to verify the authenticity of the document, he added, but if it was kosher, and it was a biggish if, then what his brother had discovered was, and I quote, 'of life-changing, earth-shattering, worldwide importance'. 'This, my dear Adam,' he had written, 'is the Holy Grail of Elizabethan letters.'

You can imagine how I felt as I read this, alone in my tiny office. I have used the example of Howard Carter once already, but suddenly I knew exactly how he must have felt upon peering in to the tomb and seeing wonderful things.

The professor had taken the trouble to type out his translation for me to read. He warned me that I should not reveal any of this to anyone at this juncture, for many and varied reasons. I valued his opinion, he being a learned Oxford don, but this, we must remember, was also personal, as it was his very own twin who had discovered it. The man's wishes needed to be respected.

The letter, which the professor had simplified by adding modern spellings where necessary, read:

My dearest Percival,

I am writing to you in Stratford with much sadness, having returned forthwith from the funeral of your friend Edmund Shakespeare, who at just 27 years was taken from us to a better place. John and Mary have lost too many of their children, and I fear this latest funeral will bring them much grief and sadness, especially because Edmund was in London when the plague took him, meaning that they could not even say a proper farewell. It must break their fragile hearts to know that their son will not be laid to rest in Holy Trinity, but instead, in the faraway, noisy, mad place that is London. Thanks be to God that Will was at least there with him. That must bring some kind of comfort, and

Will, being Will, spared no expense in sending Edmund heavenwards, with flights of angels singing him to his rest.

We actors gathered in the morning, so that we could still attend the theatre in the afternoon, and ever-generous Will had paid dear for the bell at Saint Saviours in Southwark to be rung. I swear that it was heard by all of London, Percival, so loud and proud was its song. 'Twas a spectacle to behold, and I know that Will was so moved by it all that he shed many tears and needed much consoling by us all. I am sure he hath written to his family of this, but I prithee pass on mine own respects, when you see those good people.

I have sent this letter with my friend Henry Bytheway, along with two of Edmund's paintings in a bundle, the last pictures he painted before his untimely death. They were intended for his parents as gifts, I know this, so it is my solemn duty to make sure they receive them safely. Edmund, like his elder brother, was a man of many talents. In fact, he was an even better artist than he was an actor, and this is meant respectfully. The likeness of his brother Will is exact, and shows him as we all know and love him. The other picture was first sketched when Edmund last visited home, and painted from that sketch upon his return to the city. The man astride the horse, he told me, was his father, John, and the lady with the basket, his mother. The dog is, of course, Mad Jack.

May these small treasures bring some joy to his poor parents and to his family. My love to you all,

Fare thee well!

Edward Cummings, a member of Will's happy band.

Not many things can stun me into silence. This was one of them. I stared at the computer screen for… well, the truth is, I don't know how long. It may have been ten minutes or two hours. My head was too full and items needed deleting. From the very beginning of this crazy episode in my life, it had felt as if a divine, unseen hand had been guiding me down a road of multiple coincidences and strange happenings, and I sensed my journey was nowhere near over.

Still stunned, I did what I always did to refocus my mind. I staggered into the kitchen and boiled the kettle. Tea has never been just a drink to me. It is far more important than that! I feel desperately sorry for those who choose coffee instead. They don't know what they are missing.

I eventually rang David. I know I'd sworn myself to secrecy on this one, but he was an integral part of my fully realizing this mad dream, and the only person who could take it to its natural conclusion. Without his skill, I was lost. I was convinced that I now had in my grasp the only fully authenticated portrait of Shakespeare ever created. All the others were mere fabrications, idealized fantasy pictures, or else a simple case of mistaken identity. Either that or I had just fallen for the most elaborate con trick in art history. Only Professor Ridgley the Second could clarify that.

David answered the phone. He was out of breath because he'd been counting mice at the top of his garden. I explained what had just happened and I think he felt the need to sit down.

'So,' he sighed, 'you're telling me that, after eight weeks spent at this easel, I might well have to paint the face yet again?'

He promised me he would begin cleaning the portrait immediately, and would work on it until I picked him up to travel to Snitterfield.

Chapter 12

An Unexpected Outcome

Operation Phoney Business Card went without a hitch. There was one heart-stopping moment when we arrived at the Chambers of Horrors residence (as David had christened it), thanks to the Hypnopotamus positioning himself inches from the inside of his front door, just as we were about to shovel a few cards through his brass letter box. We could make out his huge frame through the fancy stained glass, standing there in the hallway reading some leaflet or other. If he'd have chosen to open the door and talk to us at that juncture, I don't know what might have happened. Luckily, he ignored us and carried on reading, but as we scampered down his drive I did look back to see him bending down, presumably to pick up our cards, which was a good start. We then repaired to the local pub to calm our nerves and sink a large glass of red each to give us the Dutch courage required for Phase Two. A few hours later, once the writer had convincingly thrashed the artist at pool, we drove back to the house and took six Tupperware lunch boxes from my boot, each containing a family of cute field mice. We tiptoed up the drive and arrived at the front door. This time, Chambers was not cluttering up the hallway.

We could hear muffled voices and music coming from another room, so we guessed he was watching TV. I pushed the letter box open noiselessly, while David lifted the lid on the first Tupperware box. He placed it against the open letter box and angled it so that, in theory at least, the mice would scurry through the slot and skedaddle across Chambers' parquet floor in all directions.

They didn't. They just sat there, unimpressed.

David gently flicked a couple of them with the back of his hand, and two of them shot over the side of the box and into the night.

'We can't afford to waste them,' David hissed, 'or we won't have enough for an infestation.'

We tiptoed back to the car to have an emergency pow-wow. Clearly, our scheme was not working as smoothly as we had hoped. It was fraught with technical difficulties.

'We need to find an open window,' I whispered. 'That letter box is no good.'

David volunteered to go on a quick reconnoitre. A few minutes later he was back, breathless but with a smile on his face.

'There's a small window near the back of the house, in the carport area. Not sure what it is. Downstairs loo, pantry, something like that.'

We crept back up the drive with our Tupperware, nearly suffering a synchronized double coronary when a lady walked past with her dog. We waited until they'd cleared off and proceeded, David doing those silly dramatic hand gestures that are so beloved of secret agents and military types, or at least, the Hollywood versions of them. We arrived at the small window, and I silently lifted the latch up, which gave us more of a cavity – around three times the size of the letter box, and big enough to upturn an entire Tupperware container into. David opened the first tub, turned it upside down and gently shook it to remove the clingy inmates, thereby releasing at least five mice. This was better! He repeated the exercise with the other five boxes, meaning that we had, by our reckoning, released at least 25 mice into whatever this room was. I dropped the catch back onto its peg, and we shot back to the car like tiptoeing whippets, eager to start the engine and drive home. It was just then that we heard him scream, and scream he did, like a big, girly, female girl. I imagined him standing on a stool screaming with his hands either side of his florid face, like cartoon ladies did in *The Beano* upon spotting a cartoon mouse in the kitchen. Wherever we'd offloaded the little creatures, Chambers had, by sheer luck, visited this room seconds later, judging by the commotion. We nearly wet ourselves laughing, and drove off at a rate of knots, into the night.

*

The following day I was pacing the floor, nervously waiting for the phone to ring. David had added my number to the business card, rather than his own, because he figured that I had more time on my hands to answer the telephone than he did, which was fair enough I suppose. Helen rang – causing me to jump at least three feet in the air like a rocketing pheasant – to announce that she had returned from The Big Smoke. We arranged to meet as soon as possible, but for the time being I decided not to disclose any detail of the revelations that had occurred in her absence, out of respect for the surviving professor, rather than anything less chivalrous.

I replaced the receiver, and was about to make even more tea when the phone rang again. This time it was a male voice. He asked me if I was the vermin man. Personally, I would have phrased it differently but I knew what he meant. My heart leapt into my mouth and started doing somersaults. I answered in the affirmative, with a mouse-like strangulated nervous squeak.

'Ah, excellent,' he replied. 'I received your card only yesterday, and I have a job for you. It's rather urgent.'

'We'll drop everything!' I said brightly.

'Thank you, I'd appreciate it! I live in Snitterfield, not far from your offices in Stratford. I'm overrun with field mice for some reason. My name is Harry Richards, and I live at 19 Arden Close, off Arden Road. You can come today then?'

I didn't see that coming.

Neither did I expect the call, ten minutes later, from Mrs Millichip, the deceased professor's next-door neighbour, or the one from Mike and Debbie Flowers at number 28. By 11.30am I'd had calls from half of the village, but nothing from Chambers. My head was in a spin. I'd promised to rid their houses of rodents, but I knew bugger all about how to do it, even if I wanted to, which I didn't. I rang David expecting sympathy and understanding, but all I got was hysterical laughter. I could, in a way, see his point. There was something sublimely farcical about it. If the bottom fell out of the journalism world, or for that matter the art world, we could set up a legitimate pest-control business and probably do really well. It seemed that Snitterfield was alive with rodents waiting to be caught.

Then, just as I was thinking about reaching for the service revolver and ending it all, the phone rang once more, and this time it was the one we were waiting for. Chambers told me he'd been watching television and needed to take a leak, so he'd popped to his downstairs lavatory, where he was met by not one, not two, but, in his words, around 356 field mice. He'd meant to get in touch that morning but he had to go into the office early, hence the reason he'd only just got around to ringing me. He agreed to meet me at his house at 2.30pm, just to let me in, and then head off back to the bank. I was to do whatever pest-control officers do, and then slam the door behind me and report back to him the following day. I sped around to David's place, and he rushed out with two high-vis jackets, a briefcase, and an assortment of false facial hair. We got to Snitterfield bang on time and rang Chambers' doorbell. He opened the door and asked us in, eyeing my hirsute fizzog with some interest, which made me more than nervous. We asked where the mice were situated, and he showed us the downstairs lavatory, explaining that several had now escaped to the kitchen and hidden under the units in gangs. He said he was now finding little mouse poops on his work surfaces and in his bread bin. How David stopped himself from saying 'Good!' I will never know. Meanwhile, I could feel my beard becoming unattached from my chin, so I grasped it in such a way that made me look thoughtful. We promised to rid his house of mice and close the door behind us. He handed over the £75 call-out fee (which David was quick to pocket, let me add) and left us to it. As soon as he had gone, we set about searching his house, with me taking the downstairs and David the upstairs. A few minutes later, David called to me.

'Up here, quick. You need to see this.'

Whenever I hear that kind of dramatic statement, I always think of corny cop dramas. All that was missing was the word 'sarge' at the end of the sentence. I think David had been watching too much TV. I dashed up the stairs, three at a time, and followed his voice into the main bedroom, expecting to see the Shakespeare painting on an easel. Instead, I saw two beautiful, naked women asleep in Chambers' bed, in the spooning position. It took a fair bit of intense ogling before I realized that they were highly realistic sex dolls.

'Good God!' said David. 'Not one, but *two*. He's a thief *and* a pervert!'

Once David had recovered, he continued searching for his painting, while I busied myself pulling back the bed sheets, just to check if the picture was hidden there.

A minute later he found it, propped against the single bed in the box room. Mercifully, it was in perfect condition. Between us, we carted it down the stairs and through the front door, still wrapped in the tartan blanket.

'What about the poor mice?' I asked as we were leaving.

David returned to the house and opened the back door, next to the downstairs lavatory, to give the mice a chance to vacate the premises.

'What if he gets burgled?' I asked with mock sincerity. David smiled at my little witticism. We eased the picture onto the back seats, jumped into the car, and drove off towards Henley-in-Arden.

'You know,' I said as we cruised through that delightful village, 'I feel ever so guilty about not ridding those other houses of mice.'

Chapter 13

Bill the Quill

'I'm afraid Mr Hamelyn and Mr Piper suffered a very serious motorcar accident on their way to a job in Snitterfield yesterday,' I said, employing my best sombre, respectful tone. 'And sadly, because of this, the business has had to close, at least until they recover, if indeed they ever do.'

The lady seemed genuinely upset and offered her condolences.

'But what shall I do about the mice?' she enquired, quickly recovering. I suggested the *Yellow Pages*.

Within ten minutes I had been forced to repeat this pack of lies three times, and it was wearing a bit thin. I was dreading the fourth time. It came at around midday. Chambers was furious with us for leaving the house wide open, and not appearing to have done anything at all about the mice, other than extract a sizeable fee from his wallet. I may not be overly astute, but it was slowly dawning on me that our Mr Chambers was not yet aware that the painting was missing. I asked him to go and look in his spare room, where we had set traps; another barefaced lie. He galumphed up the stairs, opened a door, and then I heard an assortment of loud threats and obscenities.

'So, the way I see it, Mr Hypnopotamus Chambers,' I began, once he'd ceased the Tourette's routine, 'is that you got off lightly. Why don't you sit on the edge of the bed before you keel over, you big fat bastard, and listen to what I have to say, nice and quietly please, and you can speak at the end. Firstly, the picture you stole from David Day was not a freshly restored Elizabethan painting done by William Shakespeare's brother, as you erroneously imagined. It is a brand-new picture, painted in the old style by Mr Day to commemorate the 400th anniversary of Shakespeare's death. You left behind a business card and a betting slip, you fat moron, so we knew who'd purloined it. Instead of calling the police and having you arrested, which meant prison and losing your job at the bank, we chose to steal it back, charge you £75 for our petrol, and leave you some adorable pets to look after as a bonus. Suddenly, a few cute mice and some loose change don't seem much of a price to pay do they? Not compared to spending five years at Her Majesty's pleasure and being sexually molested every time you drop the soap in the communal shower block. And be aware that any retaliation will be met with brute force, so don't even think about getting your own back. David has worked in Italy for years, and as he would say, *la vendetta é un piatto che va mangiato freddo*. He knows some powerful people who are devils with the old cheese wire and the concrete wellies. Revenge is a dish best served cold, Mr Hippopotamus. Rub him up the wrong way again and he will have you rubbed out. He has friends in low places. As for your gambling, my advice is to seek help. My theory, and tell me if I'm wrong here, is that the gambling addiction is making what used to be a nice chap into a monster. You lost your entire fee after the Stourbridge show didn't you? You then hypnotized Professor Ridgley and got him to spill the beans on the life-changing discovery he'd bragged to you about whenever he met you at night school or in the village. You needed a lot more money to fund your habit probably, and turned to theft to achieve that aim. As to the bank, I also know about how you've been embezzling money from there too.'

'Can I interrupt?' asked Chambers. He seemed to be sobbing like a child now, so I let him butt in. I'm only human.

'I've never taken money from the bank, I swear!' he said brokenly.

'But I got everything else spot on,' I replied triumphantly. 'Not bad for pure guesswork and intuition. Mend your ways, seek help at Gamblers Anonymous, and no one will hear any more about it. Oh yes, and try keeping your feet out of the pantry. We're giving you the break you need, so don't let us down. Oh yes, and we met your lady friends in the bedroom. Lovely! I bet they never argue with you do they? Much better than real people, and both so accommodating. David and I were made very welcome!

Incidentally, can you detach their cute little whatsits when they need cleaning out?'

All I could hear now was a fat man blubbering.

'And one last thing,' I added. 'I do NOT love Eric the fucking penguin.'

I put the phone down, satisfied that I had dished out criticism and forgiveness in equal measure, even though that last bit about his blow-up women was beyond the pale, even for me. Somehow, I doubted we'd hear from Gary Chambers again.

*

I'd left David in peace to work on restoring the two paintings, as he hated to be rushed or watched over when he was at work. To say I was wildly excited about seeing them was a massive understatement, so I tried my best to stay calm and do things to take my mind off it. I was also having real trouble sleeping, because my brain was absolutely buzzing. Meanwhile, I busied myself by rekindling my romance with Helen. We'd just got back from the cinema, where we'd watched a sloppy romcom (her choice, not mine I'll have you know), and were having a nightcap prior to bedtime. Her rather nasty cold had left her partially deaf, a temporary encumbrance that wasn't without its comedy moments, even though we should never mock the afflicted. I was telling her, vis-à-vis the film, that I wasn't overly keen on the weepy bits, which I thought were a bit cheesy, and she said she quite liked them, as long as the milk was hot, and she bizarrely added that, as far as she was aware, there was definitely no cheese in them. It turned out she thought I had said Weetabix. On a different subject altogether, I do worry about female logic, I really do. I'd decided to rustle up a few sausages as a late-night feast after the cinema – we were both ravenous – and I asked her if the ones that had been in my freezer for nine months were still edible. She insisted that they'd be fine, but my counter-argument was that the label said, 'If frozen, eat within one month'.

Helen insisted: 'That's okay! It's not so much a health and safety thing – it's just that they won't taste any good after that time.'

'Oh, that's okay then,' I replied. 'They won't actually kill me but they'll taste shit!'

We eventually opted for a cheese sandwich each and a bag of crisps. Apropos of nothing, the conversation turned to how different generations had very different moral codes. For example, when I was a child, it was frowned upon to eat in the street, but now everyone does it. Our parents had this real hang-up about things we don't give a damn about nowadays, like putting your elbows on the table during dinner. Now you're unlikely to be sat around a dinner table with your family. Everyone is glued to the telly with a plate on their lap, or else obsessed with their mobile. Conversations between adults and kids, and, for that matter, kids and other kids, are also becoming a thing of the past, thanks again to the mobile phone and the earphones that come with them, and don't get me started on selfies, and even worse, the selfie stick. Maybe I'm biased, but I prefer the generation I was born into. Mind you, that didn't always fulfil the promises it made. *The Who* banged on about dying before they got old, but they appear to have changed their tune now that they're pensioners. I didn't see them skipping over to Switzerland to check in to the Dignitas clinic on their fortieth birthdays, like they promised us they would. And I'm still waiting for Toyah Willcox to 'turn thuburbia upthide down'. I must have waxed lyrical about this and other related topics for over half an hour to a woman who probably couldn't hear a word I was saying. Maybe deafness does have its perks after all. Then, at 11pm, just as we had finished eating and reminiscing about the Victorian values of our idyllic childhoods, the phone rang, and I don't know about you, but whenever I get a call at that time of night my heart skips a beat, and in the words of my dear mother, I think 'summat's up'. It was, thankfully, just David calling to announce that the restoration work was finally complete – the man put in some marathon shifts, it had to be said – and I really needed to see the results of his handiwork as soon as possible. To this end, we arranged to meet first thing the following day at his place. I'd have actually gone there and then, but Helen might have beaned me with a saucepan. In fairness, she still had no idea that I'd purloined the picture hidden behind her seascape, which could potentially now be worth a fortune.

How that would have gone down, I am not entirely sure, but you have my word that she was going to be compensated when the time was right. I am many unsavoury things, but I am not a cad!

Chapter 14

The Face that Launched a Thousand Quips

I sat staring at it for ages, transfixed. It was beautiful. David had transformed it. No longer was it a filthy torn canvas. Now, it looked as if it had been painted the day before. The colours were now as vibrant as they must have been when the picture was created, and the small rips in the canvas were no longer visible. David had done such a skilful job that I honestly couldn't even see where they used to be.

But enough of the teasing. I know you are impatient to know about the face. What did Shakespeare *really* look like? Did this portrait bear any resemblance to existing ones? Was he dashingly handsome or a plain Jane?

Well, the first thing that I noticed were his eyes. They looked at me. They were soulful and wise, and beneath them were the tell-tale bags of one who had written too many words in candlelit inns. The face was gentle and kind, not aristocratic or haughty. It vaguely resembled the famous Droeshout engraving, but lacked that decidedly odd, mean-minded, curtain-twitching, tax-official-cum-accountant look that the engraving had. If the Droeshout portrait were to possess a voice, it would surely be the irritating nasal whine of a Monty-Python-style local councillor, rather than a rich-toned and eloquent orator. Ben Jonson may well have approved it but the Droeshout engraving was still pretty awful. Maybe Jonson was jealous of his mate's work and deliberately approved a ghastly portrait to help wreak his revenge. Or maybe he was seriously myopic. We will never know, but somehow it became an iconic image, in spite of its awfulness. At best, it was a decent police-identikit version of the Bard (good enough to secure an arrest but no work of art), whereas the painting before me was real flesh and blood. Shakespeare was not textbook handsome, but equally, he was not plain or dull. The hair, whilst approximating that bizarre style on the engraving, looked natural and of its time on Edmund's portrait, with the areas just above the ears tinged with middle-aged grey. This picture was painted by a brother who hero-worshipped his elder sibling. There is no doubting that. There is also no doubting that young Edmund, so cruelly taken from us at 27, was a master painter and could easily have forged a career as one, if the bottom fell out of the acting market.

The moustache and beard combination was also as the Droeshout engraving, but the oil-paint medium helped it to appear more natural and photographic. The sitter was shown wearing a simple, soft white collar, rather than an elaborate ruff more suited to those of nobler birth. He was wearing a green brocade jacket trimmed with black piping, set against a dark background that suggested an oak-panelled room.

Suddenly, I became extremely emotional. We two new friends were the first people for who knows how many years to see what the real Shakespeare looked like. The brushstrokes a mere foot in front of my liquid-filled eyes were applied over four hundred years ago by Edmund Shakespeare, who soon after departed this earth, and three feet behind the small canvas once sat his superstar brother, posing patiently – the man who changed the literary world forever.

How Professor Ridgley came by the paintings is now known. He'd found them in a small antique shop in Henley several years previously, though how he came by the letter that led him to be interested in the pictures is anyone's guess. How the two paintings found their way to that shop, and where they resided during the 400 years prior to that is another story – a mystery that will probably never be unravelled. I turned to David and a remarkable thing happened. I began to cry.

'Don't be embarrassed,' he smiled, putting his arm around me. 'I did the same thing, strangely enough. Powerful isn't it?'

I nodded, feeling more than a tad foolish. The more I tried to stop crying, the more I seemed to cry.

'Can you see the signature?' David asked. 'It was completely covered over with the grime of 400 years. See that small "E. S." in the bottom right-hand corner? It made my neck hairs stand on end when I uncovered that. I'll begin work on the Henley Street picture next. Can't wait!'

I hated to bring up the subject, but I felt I had to, once order had been restored to its throne, and I'd dried the tears with the sleeve of my shirt.

'So how do you feel about your own painting of him, now that you've seen this?'

The two paintings were only feet apart, and his own version was quite different, facially. I could see that I had dragged him into the Slough of Despond. He looked distracted.

'Gnaaaaah!' he eventually said.

'Meaning?'

He tore at his thinning hair in frustration.

'I have no bloody alternative but to redo the face.'

'But it was approved by Stratford,' I said.

'It may well have been, but now we *know* what Shakespeare really looked like, how can I justify leaving it as it is – more like a swashbuckling Robin Hood type? The face is coming off right away. The hair's all wrong and so is the face. Thankfully, the angle of the two heads is similar, so I can virtually transplant the new likeness on top

113

and it'll look natural. Even the lighting is from the same side, which is a blessing. There's no time like the present. Off with his head. It has to be done.'

He began gently sanding down the lumps and bumps of the previous face, which was quite awful to witness. He no longer appeared to realize that I was still in the room with him. He seemed completely preoccupied. Regardless of the inaccuracy of likeness, it was still a beautifully painted face, and he was trashing it in a fit of artistic pique.

'Do me a favour,' he eventually said, stony faced. 'Go and find the kettle. Tea's in the cupboard by the fridge. Cups on the drainer.'

I did what I was told. By the time I got back, Shakespeare's head was white. He'd painted it out, ready to begin again. He still had time to paint a new face before the festivities, but the drying time was a bit tight. He didn't want it to still be wet on the 23rd of April.

Sensing that he now needed to concentrate, I drank my tea quickly and made my excuses. Once home, I packed up the letter carefully and then contacted a well-known and reliable courier firm who were tasked with delivering it to the professor in Oxford. The driver asked if I wished to insure the package and I said yes, though I lied about what the contents were. When he asked me the value of the goods, I was tempted to say 'priceless', but I didn't think he'd have a price to cover that, so we agreed on £500. He assured me that it would travel in his van straight to the professor's college, and it would have to be signed for before it was handed over, so insurance was really just a formality. I tried my best to explain to him just how important it was to me, and begged him to guard it with his life. If I'd have banged on about it much more I'm sure he'd have stolen it for himself. I bit my lip and watched him walk away with it. It was a heart-stopping moment, I can tell you. In hindsight, I should have delivered it myself. Once the man had gone, I emailed Professor Ridgley and told him to expect it. I also implored him to not let it out of his sight, and tell no one what it was, for both our sakes. He emailed back and asked me not to fret. He was used to dealing with priceless antiquities, he said. Once analysed by his boffins, he would let me know, so I could decide the best way to get it back. If it was what it purported to be, I would have to fetch it myself. If it was phoney, it didn't matter. He also gently reminded me that his brother's track record with such things was not great. The Holy Grail turned out to have come from B&Q's garden department. All this should have put me off, but it didn't. I *knew* what it was, and so did David.

*

Meanwhile, James was back from his holiday, so my nights of sexual freedom chez Eve were over for a while at least. The good news, however, was that he had found himself a job, having decided that certain aspects of university life were not for him – mainly the studying aspects. In fairness to the lad, he also questioned the point of doing a Geography, Sociology or Sports-Science degree just for the sake of it, like many of his friends were doing. He really believed that the subject should be relevant, and until there was such a thing as a 3-year honours degree in Lager and Kebab Appreciation, with an option to do a PhD on the History of Nando's, he preferred to get out there in the big wide world and earn money, which he would then spend on lager and kebabs. To this end, he had somehow landed himself a job as a gofer, or general factotum, at Lacey's, the swanky auction house where his elder sister Lauren worked as P.A. to the resident fine-art expert, Bill Fielding. This involved finding lots, wheeling them into the auction room without breaking them, wheeling them out again, and making everyone cups of coffee. It was the minimum wage, but it was a good start, and it meant that, while his mates were pursuing waste-of-time courses (that ex-polytechnics – which now called themselves universities – had invented to help fill their coffers), just so they could tell everyone they had a degree, make their parents proud, and inherit a thirty-grand debt they'd have to pay back one day for the privilege, at least young James was learning the ropes and able to buy even more lager and kebabs than his mates could.

David rang to say he had nearly finished cleaning the Henley Street scene, and it looked fabulous, but he would have to break off to drive to Stratford. He was presenting his Shakespeare portrait to the mayor and a committee of councillors for approval, and he was extremely nervous. He should have been supremely confident, being one of the country's finest fine artists, and renowned all over Europe as a picture restorer who had repaired Renoirs, cleaned up Caravaggios, and mended Michelangelos. However, thanks to him deciding at the eleventh hour to give the Bard a head transplant, in defiance of the council's express instructions, he realized he'd have some smooth-talking to do.

To make matters more difficult, until the professor's scientists had deemed the letter to be authentic, the two restored paintings were almost worthless. They had no provenance without the letter, and worse still, they may even have been just part of an elaborate hoax, far-fetched as that sounded.

I wished him well, and he promised to ring me upon his return. As Shakespeare once wrote, 'The time is out of joint. O cursed spite, that ever I was born to set it right.' I think that was the line anyway. The point being, David could have done with the timing being better, so that it enabled him to present the picture to the council *after* the letter was authenticated (if, in fact, it was the real thing), meaning that, in turn, the two restored paintings, ipso facto, would be more readily accepted as genuine. Of course, even then it wasn't a done deal. The letter could be genuine, but it didn't necessarily mean that the two pictures were.

*

There was something about David's tone when he rang me from Stratford after the council meeting that, to the sensitive, finely attuned ear, suggested that things had not gone that smoothly for him. Maybe it was the way he was screaming loudly. That and the 200-odd assorted obscenities he treated me to as he vented his spleen. It made for awful listening, especially after he had dedicated well over two months of his time to the task, sat in a quiet room, self-doubt and paranoia ringing in his ears, and driving him to the point of dementia. Eight weeks of back-breaking, heart-stopping detail, applied wearily through itchy, tired eyes, with his nose and lungs full of the stench of thinners, and his hands filthy with paint, every cup of tea, and stale, ignored sandwich contaminated with oil colour and turps, only for him to be judged and found guilty in seconds by 12 intransigent buggers in suits.

'They loved everything but his head,' he groaned, deflated and depressed. 'They questioned why I had agreed to conform to their exacting brief, shown them detailed tracings, followed by colour roughs, all approved in numerous meetings, only to then experience a moment of complete madness at the end, which resulted in me taking it upon myself to deliberately go against their express wishes in a mad, irresponsible, cavalier, eccentric way – their words – and inexplicably decide to create a new, less-heroic, less-attractive head, just for the hell of it!'

I was cringing now.

'And do you know what? I bloody well agree with them! It's like asking a carpenter to make you a bedside cabinet, and instead he makes you a bloody commode. Don't get me wrong, it's a nice commode, a very nice commode, but it's not a bedside cabinet.'

'But—'

'So now they have refused it. Either I restore the head, double quick, or I don't get paid.'

'Shit!'

'Shit is too small a word for it. Twenty grand down the pan unless I remove Shakespeare's real face and put Robin Hood's back. That head will be in 3D if I apply any more bloody paint. I can't win. I can't bloody well win! It's a painting of Shakespeare that actually *looks* like him, but nobody in the whole world knows what he really looks like except you and me, so they're asking me to make him look like bloody Robin Hood instead. Then, as soon as I've done that, you'll be in a position to showcase your proper, authentic Shakespeare fizzog to the world, no doubt pocketing a fortune in the process, and then everybody, including the council, will tell me my version is shit and the head needs to be changed again. Who'd be an artist? Eh? If I was a mathematician, they'd ask me what two plus two was, and if I'd said 'four' I'd get paid, and if I'd said 'five', I wouldn't. I could live with that, but my job—'

'So what can you do?'

'Nothing! That picture just won't take another repaint. I'm going to have to tell the council that, unless they accept it as it is, the commission is off, and I lose twenty-five grand.

I already know their answer. They won't budge, but neither will I. The difference is, it hasn't cost them twenty-five grand.'

'Listen,' I said. 'It's their loss. It won't be long after the celebrations when the professor hands me his proof. Then the council will come cap in hand, begging you for that picture. It's the first painting ever, apart from the Edmund Shakespeare one of course, to portray the Bard as he actually looked. They'll be fighting to own it. The entire world will be fighting to own it. You can name your price. Twenty-five grand is peanuts compared to what you'll be able to ask for it then. I say stand your ground.'

Bit by bit, I had succeeded in talking David down from his imaginary skyscraper window ledge. I think he could see that what I'd said made sense. We just had to bide our time. That said, I later rang Suzanne and asked her to hide the kitchen knives and the potato peeler, just in case.

Chapter 15

The Bombshell

The celebrations in Stratford had gone off as expected. Thousands of visitors from all over the world had arrived to pay their respects to the Bard, and the usually restrained, conservative Tudor streets played host to a colourful New-Orleans-style carnival. News teams from all over the globe had attended and beamed back images of partygoers wearing their Shakespeare masks. The Royal Shakespeare Company had welcomed Prince Charles and a host of big theatrical names, including Dame Judi Dench, Patrick Stewart, David Tennant, Benedict Cumberbatch, and many more (too numerous to list here), and had treated the lucky few to a posh lunch and glittering night of culture at the riverside theatre. Noticeable only by his absence was the Bard himself, or should I say, David's painting of him – one of only two authentic likenesses. There were no newspaper or TV articles about the painting, no publicity, nothing. David's painting remained in his studio – a recluse, shunned by his town's councillors who disapproved of his new 'man-in-the-street' looks. The red-carpeted, roped-off area of the huge marquee, where he should have hung for the great and the good to admire, was dismantled, and in its stead sat a plinth with a Land Rover Discovery on top of it, courtesy of the lunch's generous sponsors. Seldom had David been so pessimistic and depressed, but he knew his day was coming, and coming soon.

*

Chez Eve, the post had just arrived, so, bleary-eyed and still wearing my dressing gown, I bent down creakily to pick it up. There was an A4 envelope with *The Cutting Edge Magazine* logo in the bottom-right corner, which I had been expecting. It contained a complimentary copy that featured my article. I opened it, and read the compliment slip.

Great job, Adam. Love Melissa xxx

I noticed that the glossy magazine cover showed a photograph of a swan, with the River Avon and RSC theatre in soft focus in the background. It should have been David's painting, but after the council debacle, the magazine pulled out.

Amongst the mail there were also the usual pizza and curry house leaflets, a bank statement, and a mustard-coloured A4 Jiffy bag that had been stiffened with card inside. I opened it, and impatiently removed the sellotape that held the two sheets of card together. Out fell the Elizabethan letter and a sheet of notepaper. This was not good news. I took a deep breath and braced myself. The letter read:

Dear Adam,

Thank you very much for entrusting me with my late brother's letter. I have rather bad news. The boffins have tested it in every way imaginable, and I am afraid it is no more than a modern-day fake, though I have to admit that it was beautifully done by someone who must have been an absolute expert. The paper is vintage stock, dating back to around 1750, they tell me. Paper manufacture by that time had subtly changed in make-up from that available in the 1600s, and my scientists are able to spot this thanks to the many incredible tests they are now able to do. This alone was enough to confirm the fakery, but then they tested the ink, and it is modern, though coloured in such a way as to make it appear old. Likewise, the wax seal is of modern origin. That said, the handwriting and the language used is so good, it even fooled me. As I say, whoever did it was a master.

I am terribly sorry that I have had to disappoint you. As you can imagine, I am equally disappointed, but I did gently warn you that my brother had a track record with things like this. It appears that, once more, he was the victim of an incredibly clever hoax. Sadly, this also means that the two paintings are probably fakes, or at least, not what the letter makes them out to be. I will of course still have them both analysed for you to confirm their true origin, if you deem this necessary.

Yours sincerely,

Professor Crispin Xerxes Ridgley

Let me tell you that I have had many ups and downs in my life, but this latest bombshell made all the others pale into insignificance. I was so upset that I felt unable to move. I stayed paralysed, rooted to the spot for what must have been an hour. A fat bluebottle landed on my head and started wandering around, and I barely noticed it. Then, as I began to come around from whatever powerful anaesthetic I'd been injected with – possibly one manufactured by my own body in a desperate attempt to prevent me from jumping off the nearest motorway bridge – I began to realize the multiple ramifications of the professor's letter. First, and possibly worst, I had to ring David and tell him the bad news. He had changed the features of his commissioned painting of the Bard to those of a man on a filthy old oil painting I'd found at a car boot. For all we knew, he could have been a Tudor fishmonger called Jim, if he was indeed from that period. He may well have been a 21st-century fake, created by the same chap who faked the accompanying letter. This act of tomfoolery had cost me my pride and a grand dream of fame and fortune, but it had cost my new friend David £25,000 in lost income, and that wasn't just some pipe dream. It was real, promised money from a local authority that he'd thrown down the drain, because I'd convinced him the junk I salvaged from a mad professor's house clearance was worth a fortune.

I was about to go looking for a conveniently situated motorway bridge when the phone rang. It was Professor Ridgley (No. 2, of course). He was checking to see if his letter had arrived, and I said that it had, and I was still in shock. He felt that it was only right and proper, he explained, to ring me in person, which was nice of him. He asked if David had finished restoring the two pictures, and I said he had, and possibly all for nothing. I had been contemplating ringing David when the professor rang me, but I was not quite up to it.

Then, halfway through repeating his offer to forensically examine the pictures, his voice became strangely strangulated. I asked what was wrong, but no reply came. All I could hear were a couple of strange moans and a lot of heavy breathing. I called out to see if he was okay, but no answer came. For a moment I feared that he was about to succumb to a coronary like his late twin brother. Just as I was about to replace the receiver and phone 999, he spoke.

'My dear Adam, I am dreadfully sorry. I have dealt with the problem now. I am averse to killing any creature, it goes against my religion, but—' He gasped again and seemed to be trying to compose himself. 'I had to.'

I was struggling to comprehend what had happened. I imagined a wild tiger had entered his study as we spoke, but that was unlikely in Oxford. Stourbridge, maybe, but not the City of Dreaming Spires. Maybe it was an anaconda, escaped from a nearby zoo, which had entered the room via an air vent and was wrapping itself around the old chap's trousers. Rather than speculate further, I simply asked. The professor sounded a tad embarrassed.

'I'm afraid I have had this serious phobia since childhood,' he confessed, his voice still shaky.

'I was once stung repeatedly by a swarm of wasps, when I foolishly poked at their nest with a twig, and I ended up in hospital. Since then, if I see one, I freeze, hyperventilate; I think I may have a stroke. I have sought help but nothing so far has worked. I'm okay-ish until summer, and then I become a virtual recluse because that's when the evil things tend to multiply. I can only apologize.'

We curtailed our conversation, as I suspected he might need to go and lie down in a dark, wasp-free room for a bit.

I bit the bullet and rang David. It was fair to say that I have known happier undertakers. I will spare you the detail. Suffice it to say that I gave him the number of the Samaritans, and warned his wife, Suzanne, to hide the paracetamol and all sharp objects – something I seemed to be doing a lot of, of late.

I then picked up the forged letter and studied it with a fresh pair of eyes. I stared and stared some more, trying to work out who might have written it and what his or her motive had been. The more I pondered it, the less sense it made. If someone was out to con the literary world by faking a document that led to two faked paintings, why were they languishing in a Henley antique shop, forgotten by the world until a dotty old professor eventually found them? Was the letter a fake but the paintings real? Were all three created by the same fraudster? Why hadn't he capitalized on them by showing them off on TV? Where was the percentage in dumping them somewhere obscure, and just waiting who knows how many years until someone found them? Maybe the forensic analysis was flawed, and the letter and pictures *were* real after all! Now I was clutching at straws.

Then I had a mad idea. I found the email I had originally sent to Professor Ridgley, with the attachment. I opened it and studied the photograph I'd taken of the letter. I opened the real letter and held them side by side, allowing me to compare them, word by word, crease by crease, stain by stain.

Eureka! They were not the same document.

Chapter 16

The Sting

I rang David and told him to postpone the paracetamol sandwich. I had promising news, and evidence of foul play, which I explained to him in forensic detail. After scrutinizing the two versions of the letter, I was convinced that they were not one and the same. Whoever had been hired to forge it, he *was* a master, it has to be said. Professor Ridgley had said as much himself, but his comments were disingenuous to say the least. The letter I had sent him for analysis was, I was now sure, absolutely genuine – and composed by Edmund Shakespeare's friend. It was the letter in the Jiffy bag that I received from Professor Ridgley that was the excellent fake. It had fooled me at first, but then I noticed the various miniscule details that didn't tally with the original. The professor had committed a schoolboy error. He forgot that I had photographed the original to send as an attachment, so I had something to compare his letter to. This, to my mind at least, proved that the professor intended to steal the original and profit from it. This was an extremely sad state of affairs, especially as I had always planned to include him in my good fortune, if things panned out as I'd hoped. It had not escaped me that I had inherited the treasures from his late brother, and now the surviving brother presumably felt somewhat bitter and twisted that a total stranger – rather than himself – was set to profit from the potentially priceless Shakespearean artefacts. Somehow, it must have slipped the prof's mind that he gave his brother's possessions to a house-clearance firm, and was glad to be shut of them at the time. He no longer had any legal claim to the items, but I was still going to make sure that the surviving relative of the man who made this game-changing discovery was properly compensated. Now, I was not so sure. He had been so friendly on the phone, offering to also authenticate the two paintings. I was beginning to see why. The letter was, of course, a priceless item in its own right, but it was worth a fraction of the sum it would realize if the paintings came with it. It was the difference between holding one ace and holding all four (or three in this case, if that's not confusing the analogy).

The professor still had my original letter, which I needed back in order to authenticate the two restored paintings at David's studio. Conversely, we still had the two paintings that the professor desperately needed to complete *his* hand.

This required deep thinking. I needed to think like a chess master who plots four moves ahead, hoping that his opponent isn't five moves ahead. I put the kettle on. As Sherlock Holmes would say, this was a three-pipe problem, referring to the number of pipes he'd have to smoke as he ruminated. Only with me, it was measured by my Yorkshire Tea consumption.

The tea didn't help as much as I'd hoped, so instead I decided to walk around the block to see if the little endorphins in my head, or wherever the things lived, could be stimulated. I strolled past a house that was for sale, near the end of my street, and I noticed that the 'FOR SALE' sign had a few wasps crawling over it. This stopped me in my tracks. If I possessed a pipe, a deerstalker hat, and a violin, I would have smoked, worn, and played them in the order named. Suddenly, a brilliant idea had formed in my cluttered cranium. It was a gem! I dashed back home and rang the professor, even though it galled me to have to talk to the bastard. Thankfully, he was between lectures, so I got hold of him on my first attempt. I asked him when he was next in Stratford, as this was a convenient halfway house between Oxford and Stourbridge. I told him that I had another document that he really needed to see, and it was a blockbuster. The prof. sounded extremely interested in this, which was surprising, considering he'd just dismissed the previous one as a fake and had little faith in his late twin's business acumen. He explained that it would be convenient to meet at his brother's old house in Snitterfield on the following Thursday, as he had arranged to see the estate agent at 2pm to discuss a potential offer. He had his own keys to the place, so we agreed to meet at 2.30pm, once his brief chat with the agent was concluded. Then I dropped my bomb. I thanked him for offering to examine the two paintings, but it was no longer necessary. If the letter was a forgery, I explained, then as night follows day, so were the pictures, so David would probably just keep them for wall decoration and we'd forget about the whole thing. There then followed a lot of bluster from the prof.

'Oh, no, no, it's absolutely no trouble, love to do it, you never know, they might be worth something. Wouldn't you just like to know how old they are? They're still worth looking at...'

All of which to me was clear proof that I had been right about him. He'd probably got his ace forger lined up and ready to go, so that two weeks later he'd send the pictures back in a Jiffy bag and tell me they too were phoney. He hadn't seen my refusal coming, and now he desperately needed to think of Plan B, the slippery swine.

I said I'd see him at 2.30pm sharp on Thursday to show him the other document I'd told him about, and put the phone down. Then I rang Helen and asked if she could get Thursday afternoon off work, and thankfully, she could.

Now all I had to do was fetch the plastic bucket from up the shed, get some of my favourite local honey from the Honey Monster, ring Pat Selby, and visit the Sex Shop.

Chapter 17

Will goes Walkabout

I arrived at David's place at 8.30am, Thursday morning – the day I was to meet Professor Ridgley in Snitterfield. He'd asked me to drop by because he said he had a surprise for me. He met me at the front gate and he appeared to be growling, with his head in his hands. He punctuated this by howling at the sky and shaking his fists at some invisible protagonist.

'What's up this time?' I asked nervously.

'Gnaaaaah! Same as last time!' he replied. 'I've been burgled again.'

'Jeez! Not the Shakespeare painting again?'

'Yes and no. Same subject matter, different painting.'

'Oh no, no no no!' I screamed. 'Not the Edmund Shakespeare one.'

'Thankfully not,' sighed David, calming a little, for I had provided him with a bright side for him to look on, a small crumb of comfort in a cruel world. 'They've stolen the surprise one I'd done just for you.'

We walked back into the studio, over shards of glass. The easels were all empty.

'I came into here right after my Weetabix this morning to find that window caved in and the door swinging open in the wind. Suzanne and I never heard a bloody thing, did we?'

Suzanne appeared, still in her dressing gown, and kindly asked if I wanted a cup of tea. I thanked her and she trotted off to the kitchen to make it.

'*What* picture you did for me?' I asked, puzzled.

'I copied Edmund Shakespeare's picture for you as a surprise, so that when you sold the original you'd have your own version of it to keep. It only took me a few days because it was quite small with a plain background. I thought you'd like it.'

'I'd have *loved* it!' I said brokenly. 'But where are the others? The big 400th anniversary one you did, the real Edmund portrait, and the Henley Street scene?'

'Locked away safely in the house. After the first break-in, I became far more security conscious, but I'd only just finished your present so it was still on the easel. It's still ringing wet.'

Suzanne returned with tea. We sat down and drank it in an attempt to calm our frazzled nerves. Something told me that it would take far more than tea. Ketamine, the horse tranquiliser, would have struggled.

'Look on the bright side,' said David, once the tea had done what it could. 'At least it was only your present. It could have been the priceless ones. But who on earth did it? Who knew it was here and why that picture?'

'It's not what it was, it's what the thief *thought* it was,' I replied. 'I should have seen this coming but I didn't. I spoke to the professor a few days ago. I played along with him, even though I know he forged my letter. He still has the original but not the painting to go with it. I made it clear that we weren't going to send the painting over for analysis, which threw him, so he's probably hired some low-life to visit you and collect it. Not being an art expert, he'd have seen that, mistaken it for the real thing, and nicked it.'

'Cheeky bugger!' said David, frowning at me. 'He could well have been a bloody art expert and he'd have still nicked it. It was an exact replica of the real thing, I'll have you know. You forget that I too am an expert forger, but the difference is, I tend to operate on the right side of the law – mostly. Talking of which, I bet you any money the chap who forged the letter was Henry Proctor. He's a brilliant faker and did time for it a few years back. He lives in Oxford, where the professor teaches, coincidentally. I bet he was lined up to copy the Edmund Shakespeare paintings, once you'd handed them over for testing. You'd have been handed the fake ones back and the untrained eye couldn't have told the difference. Thankfully, I have a pair of trained ones.'

I finished my tea and promised to get in touch that afternoon, hopefully with good news. I had a plan, and it was a corker. I left David to sweep up the mess and phone the glazier, our new best friend. Indeed, it was me that gave David his number after he did a good and reasonably priced job on my conservatory.

I picked Helen up at 12 noon and we drove off towards Snitterfield, with me briefing her as we travelled. I knew she wouldn't baulk at what lay ahead. She seemed like one of those women who were game for just about anything. We drove to within a few streets of our destination and parked the car. I removed the plastic bucket and began the short stroll to the cottage. Helen replaced me in the driving seat and drove there. This is what happened next, and to make it more exciting, I've written it like an extract from a thriller novel.

At 2pm, Professor Ridgley parked his vehicle on the grass verge and walked down the garden path to his late brother's front door, letting himself in. A few minutes later, Helen arrived, parked up, and rang the doorbell. The professor answered, and Helen introduced herself as Nicki Bagnall, from Pat Selby & Co. Estate Agents. They both disappeared inside. A fly on the wall would have also spotted Adam Eve, private investigator, with his large plastic bucket, ringing the doorbell seconds later. Miss Bagnall opened the door and allowed him to come in. The door then closed, so that the fly was unable to follow what happened after that.

Miss Bagnall introduced Mr Eve to the professor, who politely informed Mr Eve that he was far too early, and asked if he'd mind waiting in his car for half an hour until the business with Miss Bagnall was concluded. Mr Eve politely refused to do this and threatened to introduce the professor to his bucket full of 'wasps' unless he sat down on the kitchen chair and stopped talking. The professor, who appeared to be sweating profusely and clutching at his collar upon hearing this, did as he was told, whereupon he was immediately handcuffed to the chair with Miss Bagnall's pink fluffy handcuffs, which, in spite of their appearance, were escape-proof. Mr Eve had already tried them out on her, just to make sure.

Meanwhile, inside the sealed bucket with the air holes punched into the lid, fifty or so bees, borrowed from Honey Monster's proprietor, Robin Greenwell, buzzed contentedly as they examined the various flowers and foodstuffs lovingly provided for them, to make sure their three hours or so in captivity weren't too stressful.

Mr Eve spoke once more.

'Good afternoon, professor. Let's not beat about the bush. I need that letter back which you stole from me, and I also need the painting you or one of your stooges stole from my

friend, David Day – oh, I see your coat is smeared with oil paint. It was you then, and the painting is now ruined I should imagine. Thank you! Well, that's put me in a wonderful mood. So hand my glamorous assistant the keys to your house.'

'I will most certainly not,' said the professor.

'Glamorous Assistant Helen, be a love and take the lid off that bucket, would you?'

The prof. began to struggle, but his sexy handcuffs held firm. He told Helen the keys were in his paint-smeared jacket pocket.

'I know where you live because it was printed on your letterhead,' said Mr Eve. 'Thankfully it's only down the road in Stratford, even though you work in Oxford. My glamorous assistant can get there in ten minutes. Where is the letter?'

The professor threatened to tell the police. Mr Eve lifted the corner of the lid a few millimetres. The buzzing sound intensified. 'Oh dear, they are angry!' he smiled. 'Where is it?' He was secretly pleased with his po-faced Bond Villain persona and was now hamming it up for all he was worth.

'It's in the writing bureau in the front room,' the professor snarled. 'Now please take the wasps away, please, I'm begging you. I feel sick.'

'So did I when you lied about that letter,' said Mr Eve. 'And so did David when you smashed his window and stole the picture he'd spent days painting, as a present for me. Now it's ruined, judging by your coat. Where is it?'

'In the car, outside, under the rug.'

'Helen, off you go,' said Mr Eve, 'and grab the picture on the way out. Watch the wet paint on your glamorous-assistant costume. Meanwhile, Professor Ridgley and I will have a brief chat. Ring me when you've got the letter too.'

And with that, she was gone.

'The sad thing,' said Bond Villain Eve, 'is that I was always going to share the proceeds with you, as I was with David and my girlfriend Helen, who owned the other painting. Now, thanks to your greed, that's not an option. I will, however, make sure your late brother gets the credit for all this.'

The professor just stared blankly at the wall. He didn't seem in the mood for a chat. Mr Eve continued regardless.

'Oh, and the real Nicki Bagnall will be here at 3.30. I rang their office pretending that I was you, and said you'd be late. I won't do my impression of you, but trust me, it's pretty accurate; I was very pleased with it. If the bottom falls out of the writing world, I may well reinvent myself as an impressionist. I fancy being an entertainer. Talking of which, there's a bloke literally opposite this place who's a brilliant hypnotist – Gary his name is – and I reckon he

could cure your wasp phobia, no trouble. Incidentally, how are you with bees?'

'Strangely, they don't worry me,' mumbled the professor, distractedly.

Mr Eve smiled one of his enigmatic smiles. Then the phone rang. It was his glamorous assistant, sounding a bit out of breath. She had called to say she'd located the letter.

Mr Eve addressed the professor once more.

'I'll just empty this bucket of honeybees outside. I get the impression you'd prefer your own company at the moment, in order to reflect on your stupidity. At the risk of repetition – I've already had this conversation with the chap across the way – I'll put this episode down to a momentary blip in an otherwise exemplary career. I won't be informing the police, as you won't about me holding you hostage in this kitchen. Good luck with the house sale. It should make you fairly well off. I'll go and wait for Helen, and as soon as she arrives, she'll pop in and take off your pink handcuffs. Look out for us on the news soon. Goodbye!'

Chapter 18

The Auction

David ran his eye over the portrait he'd lovingly copied for me. 'It's wrecked, in a word,' he grimaced. 'I'll have to paint the head again.'

'That's one of those sentences that most people never have to say in a whole lifetime, but I've heard you say that at least four times in a week,' I laughed, pleased with my own joke. He seemed slightly less enamoured with it.

We were sipping tea at his place, waiting for the BBC film crew to arrive. We had rung them to tell them about our news, and it was deemed so important that they'd sent the big boys from London, no less. Once this broke, there would be interviews almost daily with every type of magazine, newspaper, and TV channel, not only here but abroad. It was about to change our lives and we knew it. We still had to have the letter and the pictures scrutinized, analysed, carbon-dated, X-rayed and probably hypnotized as well, but deep down we knew they were kosher, and none of this held any fear for us now. David had met the bigwigs in Stratford to explain ahead of the media scrum what he was unable to explain earlier, and they apologized profusely. Not that it was their fault. I would no doubt have acted the same way if I'd commissioned a picture of, say, Santa Claus, and the artist had delivered the Tooth Fairy.

The good news was that the forthcoming worldwide media exposure would put the spotlight firmly on the little Tudor town of Stratford once more, and they would be able to boast the first-ever commissioned portrait of Shakespeare that actually looked like him, meaning that all the previous attempts – the Flower, the Droeshout, the Cobbe, and the Chandos – would see their stocks take a Great-Wall-Street-Crash-style hammering. The revenue from spin-off prints, postcards, plates, T-shirts, desk diaries, and the like, would fill their coffers for years to come, not to mention David's.

When the media descended on us, we intended to wax lyrical about the late Professor Ridgley, and his part in the adventure, tactfully omitting his brother's and Gary Chambers' seedy bit parts in the drama. And what a drama it was. I doubt that Shakespeare himself could have dreamt up something so crazy and convoluted. We also wanted to draw attention to another bit-part actor, namely Edmund, who gave the world so much, albeit belatedly. Now he could truly earn his place in the tale as a major player, instead of his usual 'third spear-chucker on the right' role. Thanks to us, he could now share a little of his brother's limelight. It just begs the question, how many of the other Shakespeare siblings were sublimely talented? What mark might the ones who died in infancy have made on the world, had they been given a chance? You seldom find that a family only has one bright spark, after all. It's all about the genes. David and I also wanted to credit the smallest bit-part actor of them all, without whom none of this would have materialized – namely Nosher, our very own version of Nick Bottom. Helen too deserved to have her name in lights, for it was she that purchased the view of Henley (or rather the crappy seascape), which was also painted by Edmund, and because of this, she too would receive a sizeable share of the spoils. That said, I still hadn't got around to telling her that I'd technically stolen the picture from her, for the greater good. I already didn't have a great track record in that department, for those who can still remember how this tale began. Helen still presumed that both canvases were found hidden beneath my harbour scene, I am ashamed to admit. I was going to have to choose exactly the right moment to broach that subject, preferably after a bottle of wine, some poncey classical background music, and a nice pie. Then there was the vexed question of whether to pay something to those that loved and lost – the car-booter, the Henley Antiques Emporium; the list is potentially endless, but you surely have to stop somewhere.

The first of many camera crews duly arrived, interviewed us, and left. The following week saw no less than 12 of them, and it was becoming difficult to retell the same tale and make it sound fresh each time. Meanwhile, scientists were working around the clock, carbon-dating, testing paint samples, authenticating bits of canvas, X-raying everything, and analysing handwriting and linguistics. In other words, repeating everything that Professor Ridgley had done, but hopefully this time handing us back the genuine artefacts at the end.

*

Several weeks later, only those who lived on Mars were unaware of our discovery, and the world was on the edge of its seat, eagerly awaiting the big auction. The boffins had announced that the pictures and letter were, in their opinion, the real deal, which was an almighty relief, after the ups and downs we'd been through.

We had agonized about what should happen next, but an auction was the only option. This might sound extremely callous to you – the idea of immediately offering these precious items for sale, rather than handing them to the nation – but put yourself in my shoes, if you can squeeze into a size nine. I live in a small terraced house and my wages fluctuate from nothing to not much. Helen, likewise, has no spare money. Grand gestures are all fine and dandy, but they don't pay the bills.

I did insist on one detail, however. The sale would not take place in London – at Christie's, Sotheby's, or Bonhams. I wanted my local auctioneers to handle it, for two reasons. Firstly, because they're based in Stourbridge, where I live, which is convenient for Stratford and Warwickshire, home of the Bard. I wanted them to have their moment in the spotlight, and besides, Lacey's is a prominent outfit with a good reputation, not some back-street dump that specializes in mouldy Hay Wain prints in plastic frames, and woodworm-riddled wartime utility tat. They even have their own resident Antiques Roadshow TV expert, for goodness sake. Secondly, my two offspring work there – Lauren in the offices and young James on the shop floor, so it would be wonderful for them. I also insisted that it was James, in his ill-fitting cow gown, who was to be responsible for wheeling in the three items and handing them to the auctioneer. I wanted him to remember that moment for the rest of his life, and not because he accidentally dropped one and broke it either! Those tense bidding moments are always televised, so he would be guaranteed his fifteen minutes of fame. Had he not allowed Nosher to kip on my best settee on that fateful night, none of this would have happened. Don't you ever marvel at how fragile these life-changing situations can be? We all seem to have a story about a one-in-a-million coincidence or a chance meeting, don't we? The only difference with this particular one is that it wasn't *one* coincidence but one after another, after another.

Sale day was electric. David, Suzanne, Helen and I had not slept a wink the previous night. We arrived at the salerooms early, and already the outside broadcast units had filled up the car park, meaning that alternative parking had to be laid on not far away. Normally, anyone was allowed to attend a sale, but because of the media attention, only interested parties and serious bidders were being allowed inside. We also noticed a few police officers hanging around, presumably to prevent someone grabbing the portrait, leaping into their accomplice's rusty Ford Cortina, and screeching off around the Ring Road with smoking tyres. That said, they'd have probably still been screeching around the Ring Road with smoking tyres hours later, trying in vain to get out of town. We locals always joke about having to throw a six to get off it.

Just like a boxing match at Dudley Town Hall, there was an undercard to sit through first, before the main event came on. David, Suzanne, Helen and I sat huddled together in the front row with plastic coffee cups, watching as various items that possessed club-footed cabrioles (whatever they are), scalloped edges, intaglio cuts, and tortoiseshell inlays come under the hammer. I found myself fascinated by the terminology. Things were kidney-shaped, cross-banded, and cock-beaded. I knew how they felt. One piece of furniture even boasted a gilt pediment Ho-Ho bird above a shell fan patera. Another had a dentil-moulded cornice. The word 'Chippendale' kept cropping up, leading me to wonder if there was some risqué entertainment planned for the interval, presumably because the camera crews were there. After an hour of this, I became au fait with gun-barrel legs, fret-cut borders, corner spandrels, ogee bracket feet, and swan-necked pediments. I knew how to identify Moorcroft (wasn't he related to Sherlock Holmes?), Royal Doulton, Wedgwood, Clarice Cliff, Art Deco and Art Nouveau, Stourbridge glass, Murano glass – you name it, I'd seen it, and all the time I was almost wetting myself with anticipation, waiting for the pictures to begin.

Then I had to sit through pictures from the English School (in other words, it's a picture of a cottage with a few pipe-smoking rustics in it and no one has a clue who painted it), etchings from Holland, a dirty old thing that was 'probably' by the studio of some bloke called Truck van der Rental or similar, and something impressionistic that was apparently painted by a bloke that went to school with Monet's sister's cousin's boyfriend.

Then, finally it was our turn, and all of a sudden men with huge professional camcorders on their shoulders appeared from all over the room, and began to film a gauche, young, embarrassed-looking lad in a brown cow gown as he wheeled in two smallish oil paintings and a letter on a tray. He held up the first frame and showed it to the now-hushed crowd. The auctioneer checked with the pretty young lady to his right – none other than my daughter, Lauren – that the Internet connection was working, and having been assured that it was, he addressed the eager audience.

'Lot number 246. Oil painting on canvas by Edmund Shakespeare, of his brother William, circa 1604. I am sure we are all familiar with the story behind this one, so I will commence the bidding. Ladies and gentlemen, we begin at £250,000. Do I have that sum?'

A hand holding a numbered card waved, somewhere farther along in the front row.

'Do I hear £255,000?'

The auctioneer acknowledged a bid from the middle of the room.

I sat in a daze, gripping David's leg until he had to gently prise my fingers from his bruised flesh. The bids rose with incredible speed. Previously, the auctioneer had warned me that he didn't know what to expect. Edmund Shakespeare was not, after all, an established painter, so in theory, his pictures would not be worth a lot. However, in this case, it was all about what the picture was of, and how it solved a great mystery after centuries of not having a face to put to the name we all knew and loved. That, added the auctioneer, took us into unknown territory.

In the time it took me to drink my tea, the bids were now at £875,000. The auctioneer was constantly looking over to Lauren now, as she took bids from all over the world.

I turned to David, who looked as if he might have recently died and been instantly resuscitated by paddles. He was biting his nails down to the wrist. Helen, meanwhile, had her eyes shut and appeared to be praying.

When it reached the magical one million mark, a mighty cheer rang through the room. Surely, it was nearly done now. The auctioneer loosened his tie and took a gulp of water. His once-steady voice seemed to be in danger of becoming a parched croak. The bids, meanwhile, rose to £1,200,000. For a moment, things seemed to be coming to a halt, before Lauren took another foreign bid, and the figure began to rise again at a rate of knots, before finally closing at just short of £2,500,000. The room erupted in spontaneous applause, and we who shared an interest hugged each other and wept.

Then, once the commotion had died down, James was asked to show off the second painting, a 'View of Henley Street', by the same artist. Suddenly, we were back on the rollercoaster ride. No one expected the street scene to fetch as much as the portrait, but it sold for a dizzying £1,175,000 nevertheless – nearly twice what the auction house had estimated. The atmosphere within the room was electric, with journalists dashing to file stories, and cameramen pushing and shoving to get the best vantage point. The final lot of the day was, of course, the letter, which was being shown on TV monitors all around the room. Bidding began at £50,000 and soon rose to £650,000. This scrap of fragile Elizabethan writing paper was, after all, the provenance to back-up the other two items, and the story that explained their creation.

At this tense juncture, Helen leaned over to me and whispered, 'That's almost as much as Dal from Wollaston Post Office charges for a special-delivery parcel!'

The bidding closed at £850,000, and once more, a spontaneous round of applause echoed around the room. Lauren folded her laptop and wiped the sweat from her brow. James gave me a huge grin and a thumbs up, and the auctioneer gulped down another gallon of water and stepped down from his rostrum to shake our hands. He told us that all three items had been purchased by a wealthy

British patron of the arts and esteemed Shakespearean actor, whose stated intention, should he be successful, was to create a permanent home for the paintings and letter in his hometown of Stratford. I could not have been happier.

We had just sold three items at auction for £4,525,000, minus the auctioneer's fees. The buyer would have actually paid considerably more than that sum, thanks to the 20% the auctioneer added onto their already eye-wateringly expensive bill. Not that I minded. I was helping out the company that employed both my kids, after all.

People began to make their way out into the sunshine, but the four of us didn't dare stand up for fear of our club-footed cabriole legs buckling. Thanks to our pre-auction pact, two of us were now millionaires, and the other two were just fabulously well off. Not a bad return from a scruffy piece of paper found in some twat's pocket.

Chapter 19

All's Will That Ends Will

Two weeks later David was manning the barbecue, desperately dodging the red-hot hissing droplets of fat that were attacking his body like miniscule and vindictive Exocet missiles. My kindly donated sausages were doing more spitting than Sid Vicious. At least they would taste good when they were cooked, as they were well within their sell-by date. I had persuaded Helen to let me throw away the ones glued to the bottom of my freezer before they killed someone. Besides, when you and your new girlfriend are both millionaires, you can afford to sling the out-of-date bangers, even though I still think she'd have preferred to donate them to the charity shop.

Meanwhile, making themselves at home on David's swanky rattan outdoor furniture, James, Lauren, and Nosher helped themselves to a slice of Suzanne's cake and a can of lager each, just to stave off the peckishness until the sausages and burgers were cooked. Nosher, his mouth full to overflowing, demonstrated how he'd inherited his nickname.

'What sort of cake is it?' he asked, spitting crumbs hither and thither. 'It'th lovely!'

'Thank you Nosher, it's Madeira cake,' Suzanne answered.

'I could tell it was your dearer cake, because it tastes great!' he replied, helping himself to another chunk.

I sidled over to David and massaged his shoulder.

'Everything good?' I asked. He nodded and grinned back at me.

'Did I mention to you about Bilston College?' he asked. I said that he hadn't, as yet, spoken of that magical town or its seat of learning. 'I had a phone call from the principal last week. He invited me to talk to his art students, thanks to all the Shakespeare publicity, so I did. Why not, I thought? I used to teach art there at the night school when I was fresh out of art college, just to earn a few quid. I'd teach nursery nurses and hairdressers how to draw as part of their HND certificates. Happy times! I always remembered the foyer there. It had the usual nasty reproductions of old master paintings – you know the kind of thing. The Hay Wain by Constable in a cheap, white-plastic frame, with the title stuck on with that nasty, blue-tape-gun text writer that everyone used to use back in the day. You remember – a self-adhesive, half-inch strip with the words punched into it in white. You don't see them nowadays.'

I said I remembered it. My dad put my name and address on my clarinet case and my flask with one, back in the '70s.

'Anyway,' he continued, flipping a sausage and getting a speck of boiling fat in the face for his trouble, 'there were all these pictures: Rembrandt – 'The Man with the Golden Helmet', Frans Hals – 'The Laughing Cavalier', Leonardo da Vinci – 'The Mona Lisa', Vermeer – 'Girl with a Pearl Earring... the clichéd famous paintings, all with the blue-tape title underneath. It was deeply sentimental walking through that foyer again last week after some forty years, and guess what? All the pictures were still there, just as I remembered them. I had to pop and take a look, and most had faded really badly, but the Vermeer one still looked decent. They must have paid a bit more for that one because the paper was lightfast. I took a closer look and nearly fell over. It was a proper painting, not a print, so I presumed they'd got themselves a very nice copy from somewhere, back in the '70s, hence the colours still looking strong.'

'I sense there's an interesting bit coming.'

'Correct! I happened to remember that I'd looked at it close up as a 22-year-old, because I was a Vermeer fan, and I'm absolutely sure it's not the same picture they had back then.'

'Why not?'

'Because I particularly remember it had a white border around the portrait and the title was printed on the actual paper, not stuck on the frame with the nasty, blue adhesive tape like the others. Funny how it sticks in your mind.'

'Perhaps it got tatty so they changed it to the oil copy,' I suggested.

'Maybe,' agreed David, 'but it somehow didn't ring true, getting someone to paint a superb copy – and it *was* superb – just to hang in a crappy old foyer with a load of cheap prints. Too expensive an exercise. So I lifted the picture off the wall and studied the back, and lo and behold, there was a sticker attached which read *Property of Bertram Jolliffe. On loan to Bilston College of Art.* That's when I started to experience the old "hairs standing to attention on my neck" sensation.'

'Why?' I asked. 'Who's Bertram Jolliffe when he's at home?'

David broke off to announce that the burgers and sausages were ready, which temporarily disrupted our little private conversation at the barbecue. The rabble descended on us in the style made popular by locusts and nicked off with everything, leaving David and me with bugger all to eat. He threw a few more sausages on the fire and started again, which at least gave us time to finish our conversation, even though I was starving and as such, struggling to concentrate.

'Bertram Jolliffe was a legend back in the day,' explained David with a reverence I had not often seen in him, especially for fellow artists. Usually he thinks he's better than most, and in fairness, he's usually right. 'He was a Birmingham chap, born around 1910. He began his working life as a picture restorer, working for Birmingham Art Gallery amongst others, but like me, he was also a brilliant painter.'

'Like you?' I asked with a smirk.

'Yes,' said David simply. 'Like me, as I said. Bert rose through the ranks of the top-class restorers and was soon working on Titians, Tintorettos, Caravaggios, and so on, as I was to do myself, many years later of course. The only difference was, I have always been legit, but Bert realized there was money to be made in forgery, which later landed him in Winson Green. Once he got out, he played it straight, but I never knew much about what happened to him after that. Remember, I was born in 1954 and he'd died by the time I was 23, so we weren't contemporaries or anything. Anyway, the upshot is, his own paintings fetch loads of money nowadays, as curiosity pieces really, but also because they're so good.'

'So you reckoned the picture in Bilston was actually one of his pieces?'

'I did, yes, but how it got there, I didn't know. So I asked the principal, Mr Painter.'

'You're kidding me!'

'That's his real surname. And he was able to explain how it might have ended up in his foyer, alongside all the tat. Apparently, when Jolliffe was let out of prison, he was given a job teaching at the college. It was well beneath him of course – given that art teachers as a class can't paint to save their lives – but he needed a job and was grateful for anything, being an ex-con. He worked there from his release until the late '70s. Now, I remember that Vermeer as being a bog-standard print when I taught there briefly, so he must have swapped it for his own oil painting just after that. The principal says he's never noticed that the picture changed, because it was the same subject matter. He'd have maybe spotted if Vermeer was taken down and Salvador Dalí was put up in its stead, but one girl with a pearl looks very like another, if you follow me.'

I nodded and rescued a sausage from incineration, shovelling it onto a bun. David was so wrapped up in his story, the food was becoming carcinogenic.

'So what now?' I asked. 'Are you planning a smash-and-grab raid? Surely, after last month's wages, you no longer need the money.'

'Ah! Well it's not that simple, my minted millionaire friend,' replied David, with that dangerous glint now present in his eyes. 'You see, I have been doing some research. In 1949, just after World War Two, The Mauritshuis museum in the Hague decided to have the Vermeer painting – which was looking decidedly tatty – restored, so they chose—'

155

'Bert Jolliffe by any chance?'

'Correct. They chose him to work on it. By all accounts he made a fantastic job of it and sent it back looking like a new one. Now here's where it gets interesting. I think that was because it *was* a new one. Just like your Elizabethan letter that the professor posted back to you, in fact. Getting that feeling of déjà vu yet?'

'What?'

'I think the one at Bilston is the real Vermeer.'

'But—'

'Think about it, Adam. Why did Bert loan a painting to a little provincial art college? He was hiding it in plain sight, where no one would have the slightest inkling that it might be real. A Vermeer – in the Black Country? He'd faked one to send to the Hague and kept the real one himself, and nobody noticed. They just thought it looked cleaner and brighter than it used to, but that's what they *asked* him to achieve, so they didn't think anything of it! Genius! Then he swaps the existing college print for the real painting – because no one there looked closely at the pictures in the foyer – and waits for the heat to die down. It was his pension scheme; don't you see? Only then he died suddenly, just like your Professor Ridgley did, and it's been languishing there ever since, unnoticed.'

'Jesus! Are you sure?' I asked, as my charcoal-briquette-like sausage slipped from its bun in shock.

'Ninety to ninety-five per cent,' whispered David. 'Now here's the big question. Are you up to stealing – sorry, no, let's call it rescuing – another priceless painting?'

THE END

Books in the David Day series:

A NASTY BUMP ON THE HEAD

Eleven-year-old David Day finds the curmudgeonly toy-shop owner, Miss Kettle, murdered in her shop. He duly informs Scotland Yard, only to bump into her in Tenbury Wells the following week.

MONET TROUBLE

First-year art student David Day is persuaded to forge a Monet painting by the mysterious Lord Hickman, but unknown to either of them, several other artists have the same idea.

VINCENT GOUGH'S VAN

An art-college murder-mystery of Shakespearian proportions, littered with psychic sewing teachers, psychotic students, and lesbian assassins.

THE CURSE OF TUTTON COMMON

David sets about trying to improve Britain's worst museum, and ably assisted by a cat named Hitlerina, he discovers an ancient Egyptian tomb in South Staffordshire.

PAINTING BY NUMBERS

Thirty-year-old David is having a mid-life crisis, made worse by the fact that his art studio has exploded, and the ninety-year-old 'paint by numbers' enthusiast he has befriended is not what he seems.

STEALING THE ASHES

Forty-year-old David Day overhears two Australian cricketers plotting to steal the Ashes, and, ably hampered by Laz, he tries his best to thwart their plans.

THE HUNT FOR GRANDDAD'S HEAD

The prequel to Nasty Bump! Daleks have invaded Brierley Bank, but David harnesses their power to see off the neighbourhood bully.

DAVID'S MICHELANGELO

David's best mate, Laz, opens a restaurant in an old chapel and asks David to decorate the ceiling with copies of Michelangelo's artwork. Then, during a visit to the Sistine Chapel in Rome, David makes an earth-shattering discovery.

THE CURIOUS TALE OF THE MISSING HOOF

Writer Adam Eve hires a pantomime-horse costume, but forfeits his deposit when he loses one of the hooves. His obsessive efforts to locate it create mayhem!

MR MAORI GOES HOME

Adam Eve's hell-raising uncle has died and left him a substantial amount of money – on the condition that he returns a rare Maori carving to New Zealand.

LOSING THE PLOT

Adam writes a sure-fire best-selling novel, only to lose his only copy of it. Can he find his stolen laptop and bring the thief to justice?

Geoff has also written a stand-alone comedy entitled *The Last Cricket Tour*, as well as the splendid, illustrated coffee-table book, *JB's: The Story of Dudley's Legendary Live Music Venue*, which charts the rise and eventual sad demise of England's longest-running rock club – a venue which played host to many of the biggest bands in the world, before they became famous.

For more information, email gt@geofftristram.co.uk

Website: www.geofftristram.co.uk